THIS WORLD
AND THE WORLD
TO COME

SIMCHA RAZ

THIS WORLD
AND THE WORLD
TO COME

HASIDIC LEGENDS
by SIMCHA RAZ

Translated by Shira Twersky-Cassel

YAHDAV

Distributed in the U.S., Canada and overseas by
C.I.S. Publishers and Distributors
180 Park Avenue, Lakewood, New Jersey 08701
(908) 905-3000 Fax: (908) 367-6666

Distributed in Israel by
C.I.S. International (Israel)
Rechov Mishkalov 18
Har Nof, Jerusalem
Tel: 02-538-935

Distributed in the U.K. and Europe by
C.I.S. International (U.K.)
89 Craven Park Road
London N15 6AH, England
Tel: 01-809-3723

ISBN 1-56062-185-0 hard cover
1-56062-186-9 soft cover

PRINTED IN THE UNITED STATES OF AMERICA

Table of Contents

THIS WORLD
AND THE WORLD
TO COME

SIMCHA RAZ

Author's Introduction

T his book evolved of a true incident. Some years back, at the conclusion of an exhausting debate between myself and an influential, well-known Israeli figure, an adamant disbeliever in "the spiritual world to come," I posed the following question,

"Even the most proven military officers prepares an alternative, a retreat plan before he enters into battle, for nothing is certain and mishap or failure may befall him. What if, at the end of a long life, you find yourself facing the heavenly court of justice and you discover that there is a final reckoning and a dayan, a higher judge? Doesn't the possibility that reward and punishment for our deeds awaits us in the realm of the spirit when we pass from this material existence trouble you at all?"

In response, he searched his pockets for a slip of paper. With disdain, he penned several lines to the effect that from that moment I would be the recipient of his share in the world to come. To seal the bargain he had someone witness the "certificate of sale" with his signature.

After a time, I was paid a visit by a young bearded man dressed in the black garb of the very orthodox Jew. He had heard rumor of that old debate. I related the incident to him as it had occured, and then he said,

11

"I am that man's son. As I grew out of boyhood and came to know my own mind, I chose to return to the observant life of my forefathers."

I was truly shaken, and I asked,

"What is your request of me?"

"That you return to me the slip of paper which my father gave to you. What is more, I wish to say to you that this pact can be likened to my offering your small son a sparkling but worthless piece of glass and in exchange taking from him a precious stone which is yours. You can see that this was a mistaken barter."

I assured him that I would consider the matter and inform him of my decision.

That very same evening, I was surprised to see this young man again at my door.

"I have come to appeal to you once more. Return the slip of paper to my father."

"I promised you that I would consider the matter; what is your great haste?"

"No man knows what the next hour brings. My father could pass away this very night. If so, his soul will approach the portals of the spiritual world berift of the mitzvot which he rightly earned while passing through our earthly vale. By his own hand, he divested himself of them when he submitted to you that 'bill of sale'."

Again, I repeated that I would consider the matter and he would have my reply within a day or two.

The very next day I had a talk with one of Jerusalem's learned scholars. He happened to show me a rare old book which recorded a tale of a man who sold his share in the next world to his friend - but in this narrative the destination of the transaction was hell, the "gehena", which he had sold. When the recipient of the 'bill of sale' passed from this life, the sale was judged and found to be legitimate.

Fascinated by this tale of the corporeal world and the

spiritual world to come, I asked to see the volume for myself. Through the reading, I became enthralled and was ensnared.

I will assure the reader that I did return the slip of paper to its author. My gain was the decision to peruse those old tomes recording homiletic tales of the great Hasidic rabbis and the saintly Jewish figures who performed wonders for the good of the Jewish soul. I would gather and reap the rich lore of these old legends and narratives of tales that were. Transcribing these with my own pen, I took great care to leave the texts in their original coin, as I found them and as related by our elders, permitting myself certain alterations of style so as to make each tale more accessible to the modern day reader.

*

Perhaps I should point out that the tellers of these Hasidic folk tales did not, as a rule, write them down or concern themselves with the orderly flow of prose. They were Jewish bards who enjoyed rather the telling and retelling of each homiletic legend, their intention to illustrate the morals and ethics of pivotal Hasidic values. Their arrival was eagerly anticipated in the Jewish communities scattered far and wide in the towns and villages throughout Eastern Europe.

Eventually these tales attained the status of true folk tales, to be told often and on any occasion – they belonged to "everyman". Evolving in a natural process of addition and change of both elements and motif, often the original landscape was altered beyond recognition. But, as a rule, the tale's vital principle and substance remain basically unchanged. Preserved for the next generation of tzaddikim and maggidim, on occasion a story has been draped in all manner of fabric, to better regale followers and the faithful who, with the passing of time, occupied a changing landscape.

The rich folk literature of Hasidism includes many

narratives of the tzaddik and his wondrous acts and of man's soul struggling to emerge from the encumberment of its corporeal cocoon. Whether transmitted through the agency of actual incidents or woven through the fabric of allegory, the direction of each tale was to transport the listener from his everyday world, usually one of gloom and melancholy, to the pious innocence and the flawless world of belief in the Almighty and faith in one's destiny - an aspect beyond the dictates of rational explanation which knows not the questioning born of doubt. Excelling in their simplicity, clear language and flexible framework, their best quality by far is a power to illuminate the spirit and convey the ethics and morality which should dictate man's behavior to his fellow man.

I offer you, the reader, a rich tapestry of unique tales and anecdotes which express a naive faith and trust in the Almighty, tzedaka and hesed; the qualities of charity and compassion, the Torah's precepts and good deeds, chachma and da'at, wisdom and knowledge. These are stories of men and women who correct their wrong-doing and reunite with the ways of the Lord, and these are tales of the gates to the world everlasting. They encompass both olam ha'zeh and olam ha'bah – the earthly and the hereafter – the world of the individual and the world of the community. I hope that the effect of these tales, their setting and their unique coin, will be to expand the reader's horizon and through a latticework of words allow all a glimpse into an unfamiliar world. This view can serve to deepen our understanding and enhance the mundane, the everyday, with the flavor and mystical favour of that complex world of righteous men and women who strove to achieve spiritual ascendance.

*

At the heart of these Hasidic folk tales were the words of either the tzaddik or rebbe himself, or as narrated by his hasidim and devotees among the people. It was natural that each succeeding generation of story-telling added a mystical enhancement to the subject of each tale. But I do not consider this a shortcoming. Rather, the stories have the inherent power, perhaps more than any other medium, to draw us close to the incandescent vital essence of these esoteric figures of Israel. When they departed this world, they abandoned us to its darkness. It was they who instructed and advised us that we too have the power within us to attain high spritual levels.

In Judaism, the saintly person is a flesh and blood figure who has broken the bounds of the material world by means of self-refinement and purification of the character traits given him at birth. Thus, he was able to take full control of his animal instincts. However, the homiletic narratives do not censor out tales of people who have failed the test. The weak who have fallen from virtue into vice pick themselves up and try again to attain spiritual heights. Again each weakness must undergo improvement, again single virtues be rewon. One layer, one level at a time, for the cost of the divine inheritance is high.

The Hasidic tale in essence speaks of human downfall and ascendance, it aspires to teach us a moral. This is a homiletic guide, if you will, to self-improvement.

*

Take care not to underestimate the homilelic tale. This is the advice of Rabbi Israel of Rojz'in, one of the best known voices of the Hasidic narrative.

It happened that "the Besh't", Rabbi Israel Ba'al Shem Tov – 'Master of the esoteric letters of the Holy Name' – the founder of the Hasidic movement, was traveling along a country road with his students. They were occupied with a discussion on matters of faith and the Jew's obligations to do the Almighty's work. Evening was coming on. As they approached a certain tree, the Besh't stepped down from the wagon and stood alongside the tree, his body beginning to sway in deeply devout prayer.

Soon the Ba'al Shem instructed his student the Admor Leib the son of Sarah, himself a great rabbinic master and teacher, to cut a niche into the tree and to set a lit candle within it. Rabbi Leib did so and the Besh't stood beside the flickering candle, whispering in reverent loving prayer, until the candle ceased to burn.

At that moment he lifted his eyes to the heavens above and called out in a joyous voice:

- I thank you, Blessed by Thy Name, I thank you, Lord of the Universe!

As the sun's glow grew faint they returned to the wagon. The moon made its appearance. After a quiet time, the Besh't roused himself from deep contemplation and said,

- Blessed be the Lord's name, blessed be Name of Him who has rescued our brethren Israel from a malicious decree which, G-d forbid, was to descend upon them!

Only then did the students of the Ba'al Shem Tov learn that by virtue of the lit candle and their Master's prayer a turbulent evil which had been fermenting to come upon the world had been annulled.

The Besh't and his pupils descended from the wagon and in the light of the moon's luminence they raised their voice in song and lifted their feet in exultant dance.

- Yeshuot and nechamot to our Jewish brothers, deliverance and consolation!

Many years later, Rabbi Dov Be'er, the Maggid of Mezhirech, related this very same tale within his close circle.

On a journey, he too descended from the wagon and near to an oak tree enjoined one of his pupils to carve a niche in the tree and to place a lit candle there. Thereupon he proceeded to lift his voice and direct prayer in great longing, that it might sanctify its purpose.

16

- Master of the Universe! It is well known to you that I am not able to achieve the high level of devout intention as was Rabbi Israel Ba'al Shem Tov. Therefore, I beseech you to adhere to me his merits, as though I too were capable of performing the wondrous acts and devout intentions according to the combinations of the letters of your Holy Name and thus remove the evil edict from your righteous people, Israel.

And again we find this tale, as related by Rabbi Moshe Leib of Sasov.
During a journey in the company of his colleagues and disciples, Rabbi Moshe Leib instructed that the wagon stop near an tree along the road. He then proceeded to tell of the burning candle placed in the tree, by which means both the Ba'al Shem Tov and Rabbi Dov Be'er, the Maggid of Mezhirech, removed malevolent decree from the Jewish people. Then he said,

- Dear colleagues, the saintly Ba'al Shem Tov knew the esoteric secret of the lit candle and its great power in the matter of wondrous acts according to the letters of the Holy Name and devout intention. And Rabbi Dov Be'er also knew this secret which now eludes us.

- We are a generation of tainted hearts, the most extreme of orphans and do not understand those esoteric truths by means of which our holy rabbis worked their power in order to remove evil edict which threatened the seed of Father Abraham and Father Jacob. Would that the Almighty will bless us with His compassion and that in the telling of this tale of the merits of our rabbi's power, we too can succeed to cancel malicious decrees from our brethren.

Rabbi Dov Be'er, the Maggid of Mezhirech, of whom we spoke above was asked: Where can the fervour to worship and to do the work of the Almighty, be found? And he replied,

17

- One must search it out as one searches for a spark concealed in the dust.

This reminds us that man must be humble as the ashes and modest as the dust. This is a great axiom of Hasidism: the spark is hidden in the dust!

In our day, people are not prepared to be as ashes and as dust. Is it that they they refuse to bend their will in order to search out the spark of embers in the dust? But, perhaps they can be tempted to do so - in a positive way.

This is a task that the homiletic folktale can do well by presenting the mystical figures of Israel, their wisdom of soul, greatness of heart and simplicity, in a frank and open manner.

To readers who will consider these tales naive stories of wonderment and miracle suitable only for children, I say this. There are two kinds of dancing: that which elevates the dancer though it be one small measure above the ground; and that which is a mere exercise of feet chained to terra firma.

The latter is a waste, for the dancer only wears down the soles of his shoes. In this book, I have appealed to the first dancer.

Simcha Raz

Translator's Note

Simcha Raz's book of Hasidic Tales is not only a picturesque voice out of the past. These powerful narratives transmit to the reader the fine elegance of the Torah and its beautiful discipline of faith and morality granted the western world by the Jewish people; a discipline alive and well today, notwithstanding the winds of change. It is, therefore, suitable that the thriving ethos and unique values depicted by the tales in this book be presented in as real a fashion as possible.

Translation being the imperfect occupation that it is, the measure of authenticity can be achieved only by the application of a well thought out technique. I chose to apply several translation tools not commonly in use. Firstly, I worked in an out-of-date English, evocative of the idiom spoken by a people for whom Hebrew is a holy tongue – on the Almighty's lips at the time of Creation. Secondly, I retained Hebrew terminology within the flow of text, utilizing an expanded glossary at the conclusion of the book. Thirdly, I elucidated chosen complex concepts of Torah and hasidic tradition rather than flatten or eliminate them.

I believe that readers will welcome these soul-and-heart-moving tales, and take as much pleasure in this book as I have in working on it.

Shira Twersky-Cassel

THE GATES
OF FAITH
AND PIETY

Master of Pious Faith

O nce a certain zaddik rebbe said to one of his hasidim, - If you wish to learn the trait of reliance on the Almighty, go to see a certain wealthy but modest man from whom you will learn how to cherish this trait and observe to what unlimited heights man's soul can aspire.

The hasid agreed and set aside a time. In the interval, he made ready for the far journey.

And so it was. The hasid returned on the appointed day and his rebbe gave him the ma'ot for his travel needs, enough to suffice until he reached the city of Berdichev, instructing him thus,

- Search out this particular gevir and say to him in my name that I have asked that you stay at his home. Observe him with a discerning eye, as this prosperous gevir is humble and his deeds are unperceived. From your host you will understand the direction for your own soul. You will become a master of pious faith.

The hasid traveled to Berdichev and searched out the home of this wealthy Jew. His host welcomed him with great honor and set aside a special room, saying,

- All your needs are upon me. Tell me, what do you require?

- I must tarry here for several days in connection with a confidential matter which the rebbe has assigned to me.

During an entire week, the hasid observed the gevir as he conducted his household in the manner of the grand and the wealthy, for his business dealings were very many, and every day notes for large payments were presented to him from far and wide. He always cashed each on its due date.

The hasid was very surprised. He observed no pious reliance on the Almighty in any of these things, since all his host's needs and affairs were secured by superb wealth, and many servants were needed to record these transactions in numerous account ledgers. He had also seen his host distribute charity daily, literally without measure.

Not yet understanding his host's ways, he did observe that the keys to all the rooms were given over to loyal servants, with the exception of one key which his host kept to himself. This he relinquished to no man.

The hasid asked the servants,

- What is concealed in that locked room?

- That is where the wealthy man's treasure is. He permits no man to enter there.

For one week the hasid was confused in his thoughts, pondering in his heart, "Perhaps this gevir is possessed of a true reliance on the Almighty in all things. But how can I learn this trait from one who distributes so much to charity when I myself do not possess even the smallest part of such commodity?"

And since the hasid's silence would not serve to instruct him in the direction of his soul, nor would he thus become a master of pious faith, he made up his mind that he must speak to his host, as follows,

- I disclose to you a hidden secret of my heart . . . Our rebbe has sent me here to learn from you the measure of

24

devout reliance on the Almighty. I ask, therefore, that you reveal to me the meaning of your endeavors, because at the cost of much money and effort have I come to this place.

Only then did the wealthy man offer entry into the room for which he alone held the key. Locking the door behind himself and his guest, the gevir said,

- I pray you, search out all the hiding places of this room. For here is my treasure house, and from here I cash in all payment notes, distribute charity and pay the expenses of my household.

The hasid, who strived to be a master of pious faith, examined the entire room but observed only a chair, a table and a small chest. There was nothing more, and the chamber was empty of all furnishings. Then his host opened the small chest. Inside, the man could see only notes for payment and a great many ledgers to record these transactions. The hasid himself searched the chest, but to no avail.

His host, the gevir, said,

- Know that all the members of my household and all my servants believe that this room holds concealed treasure and that I take gold from it. But the truth is that I am a beggar. I own nothing, except for my devout trust in our Creator, and it is that pious faith which provides all my needs. When in need, I am accustomed to lock myself in this room. I sit on the chair and I speak with a heart humbled and brought low to the Creator of the Universe. I say to Him,

- "Almighty One, such and such is my lack on this day. My faith is strong that you will help furnish me with money in this hour so that I do not fall short, G-d forbid, and in order to pay my debts." And truly, the good Lord provides on that day. . . Perhaps you have observed my custom that not one kopek rests in my pocket overnight. Every day, on that very day, I distribute every extra ruble and each silver kopek to charity. I do this because I am certain that on the morrow the blessed Almighty again will sustain all my needs. O' yes, it was not for naught that the rebbe sent you to observe my behavior, for I am steadfast in my reliance on the blessed Almighty."

As they were conversing, a voice sounded at the threshold. His host left the room to meet a messenger who came to him carrying a payment note from his gentleman to the sum of several thousands. And he said that his master awaited payment.

The gevir instructed the messenger,

- Please wait until evening.

Then he re-entered the room, saying to the hasid,

- Now it is time for me to repay a large debt of three thousand rubles. My faith in the blessed Almighty is firm that He will help me pay my debt this evening, and that is when I appointed the messenger to return.

You who hear this tale, let us observe the wonders which the Lord of the Universe performed.

As his host perused his ledger to note the exact sum necessary for payment to the owner of the promissory note, suddenly the servant knocked on the door, announcing the arrival of a certain gentleman. The gevir asked that the visitor enter. It was an important commandant of the regiment, on his way to the war front. At that time there was a war raging between the Yaktarina empire and the city of Atshakov. The commandant addressed the gevir,

- On this very day, I have been dispatched to the place of war, to the city of Atshakov. But, I have with me the sum of ten thousand gold coins, and no desire to carry this money with me to the battlefield, lest I die there. For I am without progeny, and to whom can I leave this fortune? Therefore, I implore you to accept these ma'ot for safekeeping. They are in your hands and there they will stay until I return from the war. If I return alive, one thousand gold coins will be your earnings. But if, G-d forbid, I fall in battle, I declare charity of

Prayer – H. Struck

my money. And as charity from you and from myself it will be considered, gaining virtue for us both in the life to come. I appeal to you because I know you as a loyal, honest and beloved man.

The gevir agreed to serve as trustee for the commandant's ma'ot, and wrote him a receipt noting, "Received, nine thousand gold coins in trust for this certain commandant until his return from the war and one thousand reds as payment for my commission," and so on. Accompanying the commandant to the door, he blessed him that he might return in peace from the battlefield.

The hasid studying to become a master of pious faith observed all these things. Then his host turned to him,

- Now you have seen with your own eyes that the deliverance of the Almighty is swift. This should be more than enough for you to learn the trait of reliance on the Lord. Such should be the life of man and woman in the temporal world, to be firm in their faith in the Almighty with the certainty that only the Almighty can help and rescue us. Now, go. Return to your home for it is time, and the compassionate Lord will strengthen you in your confidence in Him.

However the hasid's replied,

- The last coin has gone from my pocket and I have not one kopek with which to travel home.

- Here are two hundred gold coins for your journey, but I can see that you have not yet learned to depend on the Almighty in all things.

The hasid wishing to be a master of pious faith accepted the ma'ot, and set out on his journey in peace.

Traveling along the way in his wagon, he contemplated with amazement and confusion all he had seen, until there there he heard a wailing and a shouting noise arise from a place not far off. He and his wagon pushed quickly forward, and soon he came upon two Jewish women who were being led along the road in fetters by several angry guardsmen. Behind them trailed their small sons and daughters, all wailing and weeping copious tears. The hasid drew near and asked the women,

- Why do you weep and where are you being led by these guards?

The sobbing women told him that their husbands were in debt to the prince of the estate for rent of their land parcel.

- We have no money, our husbands have run off and escaped. Now the guards take us prisoner, and such is the custom of the country Poland.

The compassion of the man was aroused and he said to them,

- I will redeem you.

He demanded that the guards lead him to the estate manor, where he would pay these people's debt. When he arrived there he presented himself to the clerk,

- How much is their debt?

- One hundred and fifty reds and fifteen gold coins.

The hasid implored the collector clerk,

- Perhaps you will accept one hundred and fifty reds?

The clerk explained,

- I cannot do this, since I have already suffered much by cause of these paupers. Several times have I let them go free, although I am not the lord of the village and only his clerk collector. The prince, my lord, is a very cruel man, but not once has he ordered me to instigate injury against these Jews. Until this time, I pitied them, saying in my heart that perhaps they would somehow be rescued. . .

And he continued,

- Indeed, I protected the husbands of these women by permitting them to slip away. Now, if I tell my master that the husbands have flown, he will surely pass a death sentence on the women and their sons and daughters. And, the prince has told me that if the Jews do not redeem the debt weighing heavily on them, this time their fate will be an evil and bitter one. In short, I cannot accept one kopek less than two hundred and fifteen gold coins.

- But, I have only two hundred with me.

- Not enough!

Finally the hasid had no choice but to give over to the lord's collector all the two hundred gold coins which he had been granted him by the gevir. He submitted to him, as well, his tallit and tefillin and several other valuable items in pledge for the debt of fifteen remaining gold coins.

Thus did the hasid redeem these prisoners, the women and their sons and daughters, who happily returned to their village in peace. He did not await their gratitude, but set out immediately for the journey home, bereft and divested of both tallit and tefillin. Going along in a dejected way in his wagon without his property and without money he recalled the words of the gevir when they had parted. This thought strengthened him and he was carried aloft by a great surge of courage which fortified his conviction that the Almighty would come to his aid. Thus heartened, he now felt himself a true master of pious faith.

At nightfall he arrived at a hostel in the city of Malnik and he rested there. On that very night an honorable guest, an important merchant, arrrived in the city to conduct business in the royal manor court, and the two men shared the same chamber. Conversing one to the other as men do each asked the other, "From what city do you come?" and so on.

The master of pious faith told the merchant,

- From the Polish city of so-and-so.

The merchant pressed him, asking,

- And what is the name of your father?

- What is your interest in the name of my father? If I tell you his name will you know him?

- Know that at one time I resided in your city. It is now many years since I have parted from there.

The hasid told him that his father's name was such-and-such.

- Oh, I knew him well! . . And you my son, what is your business and what is your occupation? And where is your older brother at this time?

In this manner the merchant inquired after the health of the hasid's family. The master of pious faith replied to all these questions and related the progress of his travels. All that night they talked about many things. Finally, the merchant told the hasid,

- Since you are to journey home by way of several towns which you must enter on your way, therefore, I ask a small request of you. In one particular town, I know of an honest man and his name is as I will tell you. I dispatch to him his share of an inheritance left by a relative, of blessed memory, whom we have in common. Our late relative has died without progeny, and until this time I have not come across a trustworthy person with whom to send this heir his money. To dispatch the ma'ot by post is out of the question since I have no exact address. Therefore, when the Almighty called you to my side, I examined your countenance — you are an honest and trustworthy person. I entreat you to perform a mitzvah. Take this from my hand and thus grant life to a man's soul, whom I have learned is poor and knows nothing of his inheritance. I will describe to you how to trace and to ask after him.

The master of pious faith agreed to carry this inheritance to its rightful heir, secreting the ma'ot safely inside his clothing. The merchant offered the hasid several more hundred gold coins for the journey, but he refused them. After much urging and entreaty the merchant finally said,

- These ma'ot I give you as a gift. Then the hasid took the ma'ot from his hand and went on his way.

When he arrived at the city of which the merchant had spoken, the hasid asked and searched for this heir in all the city, but no one had heard or knew of him. Speaking to the town elders, they would only say,

- You are mistaken. There never was such a man in our town.

The master of pious faith tarried in that city for several days, but no one spoke and no one could help him perform his mission. Unhappy, and not knowing what to do with the money which the merchant had entrusted to him, he left that place in disappointment.

He arrived well and in peace to his home. After resting for several days, he went to his rebbe and related all that had befallen him, from the first day to the last, and of his regret and sorrow that the merchant had trusted him with an inheritance to deliver to a man who could not be found.

Then the rebbe said to him,

- This ma'ot have come into your hands as a result of your pious faith. For there never was such a man in that town for whom you searched. And the merchant who entrusted them to you was not a flesh and blood man at all, but the angel who comes into the world born of the mitzvah of redeeming captives which you performed for the women and their children. Of the many fortunes created by the Holy One Blessed be His Name, one fortune has been revealed to you by reason of your pious faith and embracing trust in the Almighty. Now the money is yours, to do with as you choose — whether it be to give charity or to perform other benevolent acts for your brethren Israel. Your faith has truly been strengthened by the matters which you observed at the home of the gevir to which I sent you.

His rebbe continued,

- The Almighty will be your sustenance, as all things emanate from Him, including the very power to elevate man's level in faith. We must be fortified in this particular trait. My teacher, Rabbi Israel Ba'al Shem Tov, of blessed memory, guided me thus. And he said, "The celestial court cannot punish one who is certain in the quality of faith in the Almighty. If such a person must be punished for a severe cause, his trait of faith is taken from him."

- Go and be strengthened in the Almighty. He will be your assurance and persuasion always, your feet will never stumble or your heart waver along your way.

The Almighty
Forsees The
Generations

A true story of our teacher and master, Maran Rabbi Israel Ba'al Shem Tov, of blessed memory, who was traveling through a desolate steppeland accompanied by one disciple hasid. They journeyed several parasangs but found no water, and the hasid was greatly thirsting, so much that he felt that he was dying.

- Our righteous rabbi, I greatly thirst!

The Besh't did not address him. The hasid, fearing that the cause of his suffering was soon to bring about his death, called out, - Rebbe, I need water for my life is in dire danger.

Then the rebbe spoke,

- Do you believe it possible that in the instant the Holy One created the world, he did not anticipate this trouble would come upon you and prepare water to drink?

The hasid disciple thought for a time, and soon he recovered his reason,

- Our rebbe, I do believe it !

The Besh't, of blessed memory, then proposed to him that patience be their watchword. Journeying on for a short distance more, before them passed the figure of a servant balancing two leather waterskins on his shoulders. Once at their side, he agreed to sell them of his water for several pennies.

Our pious master then asked the servant,

- How is it that you carry fresh-filled waterskins across this deserted steppeland?

The water-carrier replied,

- My lord of the manor lost his mind! And although we have much water at the manor, and he has sent me to draw water from a far-away spring. This is why you find me carrying this skin from a distance of three parasangs. Believe me, I do not know the why.

Hearing this, our teacher and master said to his disciple hasid,

- Observe the Divine Providence of the Blessed One. For your sake has He created a manor lord who lost his mind. Thus the Almighty, in His Providence, anticipating this event from the instant that He created the world, devised water for you to drink in this barren place.

A Celestial
Partnership

This is a true tale which occured during the time of the Gaon Rabbi Abraham Yehoshua Heschel, of blessed memory, author of the "Ohev Yisrael". In a certain town near the city of Rabbi Heschel, there was an Israelite shopowner who made his living from the sale of alcoholic drinks, such as chnapps and wine for Shabbat kiddush. After some years, it was reputed that this man was able to perform wonders; that all who came to him would be made well and saved from any trouble. The ill were cured, the poor became wealthy, and regarding other kinds of misery, the blessings and comforting words of this shopowner always brought ease and remedy. It was a wonderment in the eyes of all acquainted with this shopowner, since he was but a simple man. How was it possible for such a one to influence fate in such matters, usually given into the hands of the spiritual greats of Israel?

Word of this reached the province of the extraordinary Zaddik Rabbi Abraham Yehoshua Heschel, of blessed memory. Hearing all this, the rebbe thought to himself, "I will disguise my appearance and traverse to the city where this man is said to live. There, I can observe his actions for myself – whether he be a naive holy person or, G-d forbid, an agent of the dark powers, the Sitra Achra. If the influence of this man does originate in the supreme source of evil, I must surely obliterate his name from the world."

Immediately, Rabbi Abraham Yehoshua Heschel traveled to the city of this shopkeeper. He entered the shop and sat close by to the wonder-doer for three full days, during which time he noted no thing in the shopkeeper's behavior to indicate the zaddik or hasid. Nothing tipped the scale to the aspect of holiness. On the other hand, it did not appear to the rebbe that this man had powers emanating from the evil of the sitra achra.

What he did observe for certain was that the shopkeeper conducted himself in the pure manner of Judaism: he wore his tefillin and prayed as was the custom of all Israel. Everyday he would stand behind his shop counter selling chnapps and other intoxicating drinks. And he did not stir from his place all the hours of the day.

The rebbe considered in his heart, "Perhaps in the night hours this man worships his Creator with a unique, abiding love."

Therefore, he decided to conceal himself that very night in a room near to the bedroom of the shopkeeper in order to observe him. He saw this simple man lay down to sleep from the evening to the morning. He rose at dawn and washed both hands in the ritual manner to purify them after sleep, taking himself off to the synagogue just as do all the fine souls of the house of Israel. The rebbe wondered and again considered. Now he was certain, for it was as bright as the light of the sun, that the powers of this man did not originate, G-d forbid, in the unholy or the profane.

Rabbi Abraham Yehoshua Heschel disclosed the purpose of his presence to the shopkeeper,

- I am the rabbi of the town of Aphtah and I came here to examine your actions, to learn where have you achieved the

Rabbi with Talit, Tefillin and Torah – Marc Chagall

power to work terrible and awesome matters. If you disclose your secret – good and well. But, if you refuse to speak of your own free will, I hereby decree by the power of the sacred Torah that you reveal your secret to me.

The shop owner began to tremble, and replied immediately, - I know it is a mitzvah to attend the words of our wise men, but know, sir, that it would take much time to disclose to you all the many events which overtook my life. So, I will explain briefly. . . The most important mode of my behavior is my ever-increasing trust in the Master of the Universe. For I have always been blessed with a strong faith in the Almighty, accepting each wave of the many storms which overtake one in a unique manner. My measure is such: at the moment when I find myself in the greatest difficulties, straight away I begin willingly to distribute everything at my hand's reach to the unfortunate and to the poor. I do this with a bright and happy face. And my habit is also to host many guests in my home.

- . . . The history of my tale is as follows: My situation was very difficult and matters worsened until I was forced to sell off all of my fortune and property. Each day my resources dwindled, until I remained as berift and unclothed as G-d's creatures. The members of my household wept and implored that I traverse to another town. Perhaps there I would come upon an income, or happen upon a partner to share a business venture. I refused to heed them, because my faith in the Almighty was firm – that He would help me with a solution to our dilemma in my home town. But, my household did not give me rest, entreating every hour. The day came that their unhappiness was so great that I agreed to travel to another city where I might the find means to support my household.

- As I departed the town limits and was walking through the fields, I was prompted to raise my eyes aloft to the firmament. I found myself weeping, and soon my heart grew light. Then I heard my voice address the Master of the Universe directly,

"You who are Lord of all Your creatures, You watch over all things and provide succor for all life that you have created. Everything is revealed and known to You. . . Now, I find myself in an hour of great distress and beleaguerment. My wife and my sons and daughters have urged me to seek out a partner, a mere man whom You formed of the dust of the earth. One who is here today and tomorrow buried in his grave. Blessed Almighty, this is not my inclination. Instead, I ask that You become my partner and send down Your blessings to me. You are my witness that from this moment, I ensure to share half of all my earnings and income with You, whether great or small. That is to say, your half I will distribute to those who sit and learn Torah, I will open the doors of my home to guests and to the poor. The other half of the earnings you bestow on me will be for the needs of my household and myself, to keep our souls alive. Thus we will depend on Your bounty from one day to the day that follows."

- As I wept from without and from within the very chambers of my heart, my hand happened to touch my purse, and suddenly I was reminded that there was one remaining silver coin in my pocket. Immediately, my heart was reinforced. Returning home, I said to my wife, "Thanks be to the blessed One, for I have found myself a proper and satisfactory Partner."

- After that, the Holy One showered His blessing upon me. For example, one time, as I rejoiced with my guests, a messenger arrived from the prince of the town's estate commanding that I appear before him that very day. If I refused, the prince threatened to punish me with the most severe punishment. I thought in my heart, "I am occupied at this time with the mitzvah of hosting guests in my home, a trait which our rabbis and sages greatly valued. Certainly, by virtue of this holy deed I will be protected." Therefore, I did not leave my guests, and did not respond to the command of the manor prince. I did not abandon my guests and appear before him. After a while, when I did appear before him, I found that I pleased him. He showed me a smiling face and many pleasant things happened there.

- But, the most important of all was that the Almighty eased my lack of money. Now look and see here! I have under my hand two drawers. In the one I place the share which is mine, and in the second the share owed to the Almighty. When I redeem monies, it is never through a third party, be it a member of family, a neighbor or any other person. Only I myself redeem monies, and I take care that no one casts their hand into my celestial partnership, G-d forbid. This is the reason I do not stir from my place behind the counter all day. My prescription is that the Almighty's share is distributed to the scholars of the Law, the students of the Torah, to the decent and G-d fearing poor, and to the Jews who take upon themselves to care for the needs of the community. I do all this with a pure heart and only for His sake.

When Rabbi Abraham Yehoshua Heschel heard these things, he turned to those gathered in the shop and said,

- Do not wonder regarding this man's power to heal, for it is simple justice.

Then Rabbi Heschel quoted in the name of the Ha'ran, Rabbenu Nissim, of blessed memory, "Regarding one's partner – what he does is considered done." For according to Jewish Law, if one partner performs a transaction in the name of the partnership, even though his partner has no knowledge of it, this transaction is considered binding. According to this, the person who enters into a partnership with the Holy One Be His Name, in honest trust, innocence and devout faith, will certainly be granted the superior ability to perform wonderous acts.

42

Concentrate with Joy on the Almighty

This is a tale of Rabbi Levi Yitzchak of Berdichov, the advocate of his people, who was well known as pleader of Israel's case before the Almighty. Now, it was Rabbi Levi Yitzchak's custom to conduct the seder table on the first evening of Passover with infinite devotion and according to the Law in all its holy intentions. Thus was each Divine saying and the letters of every injunction enacted. Thus did the secret and latent meanings of every law and custom of Israel shine their countenance on the bright festive table of this excellent zaddik.

One year, at the conclusion of the seder at break of dawn, Rabbi Levi Yitzchak retired to his own chamber, his heart replete with the joy of an exemplary seder. Suddenly a celestial voice addressed him, saying,

- And what exactly is it that you are so proud of? . . . I have more affection for the seder conducted by Chaim the water-bearer than for your own!

Then Levi Yitzchak immediately called for his family and

his students to ask who was this man, Chaim the water-bearer. But no one knew of him.

Then the zaddik instructed that several of his student disciples seek out this person. Wandering the city for quite a time, finally they came to the poor section at the edge of the city where the house of Chaim the water-bearer was pointed out to them.

They knocked on the door and a woman emerged, asking what it was they wished. When she heard what they had to say, she was very surprised,

- Yes, Chaim the water-bearer is my husband. But, he will not able to accompany you to the rabbi. You see, last night he drank too much wine and now he is lost in a deep sleep. Should wake him, he would be unable to carry his legs from this place.

The students, replied,

- The rabbi has commanded it!

Entering the sleep chamber, they shook the man awake. For his part, he merely rolled two drunken eyes up at them, bewildered as to what was required of him. His only wish was to remain in his bed. Nevertheless, he was lifted away from his mattress, and supporting him with their arms, the hasidim half carried him all the way to the rabbi's house.

Rabbi Levi Yitzchak instructed that a chair be set down close to his own, and the water-bearer sat bent over in silent discomfort. The zaddik inclined his head towards him, asking,

- Dear Reb' Chaim, to which secret divine intention did you aspire when you set about examining the house for any remaining hametz in anticipation of the seder?

The water-bearer peered at him, his eyes uncertain, then seeming to nod his head, he replied,

- Rabbi, I looked into every corner, and then I gathered

Seder Night

together the remaining crumbs of hametz into the palm of my hand.

Still perplexed, the zaddik continued to question,

- And what divine intention did you attain at the time of the hametz burning?*

The man considered in his heart, then sad and ashamed, replied,

- Rabbi, I forgot to burn the hametz. Just now, I recall that the small bundle of hametz is still waiting beneath my ceiling beam.

When Rabbi Levi Yitzchak heard this, he began to doubt, but out of his dilemma he persisted,

- And now, please tell me Reb' Chaim, in what manner did you conduct the seder?

This question lit a spark in the water-bearer's eyes. He spoke apologetically.

- Rabbi, I will not conceal the truth from you. I have heard that it is forbidden to drink whiskey, which is leavened, during all the eight days of the Passover festival. For this reason, I drank sufficient whiskey on the morning of Passover eve, when it was still permitted, to maintain me through all the eight days of the festival. All that drink caused me to fall into great weariness and I fell asleep. Until my wife woke me, with the complaint, 'Why are you not conducting the Pesach seder as all Jews do?'

- And my reponse to her was,

- "What is your wish and what do you want of me, a simple uneducated man as was my father before me? I do not know what I am bidden to do and what is forbidden to do, nor how to conduct the Passover seder according to the halachah. But there are two things that I know for certain: that our fathers were prisoners in the hands the Egyptians; and that Israel has a Father in Heaven who delivered us out of slavery into freedom . . . And look, here, now again we have become slaves. But I know and am certain, and I say to you that the Holy One Blessed Be His Name will remove us from this place. He will return us to the freedom of our own land".

- Suddenly our table was set and prepared before us. There was a gleaming tablecloth white as snow, and on it a matza platter, hard eggs, all the specially prepared dishes for Pesach; and a new bottle of red wine for the kiddush and the four cups each person must drink that night. My wife and I ate happily of the matza and the eggs, and sipped the wine. A great joy filled my being, I lifted my glass to the heavens and called out,

- "See here, my Lord, I drink this glass to You ! At this moment, as You incline Yourself in our direction, hear our pleas and deliver us from this exile !"

- In this way, we ate and drank and rejoiced before the Almighty. After this I lay down in my bed and I fell asleep. And that is where your hasidim found me.

---

* - After the house has been cleared of all leavened foods, a small portion is taken to be symbolically burned to ashes.

THE GATES OF LIVELIHOOD

The Three Laughs

The Ba'al Shem Tov sat with his hasidim at the Shabbos evening festive table. After kiddush was said over the wine, the Besh't was heard to laugh a laugh so boundless that for a moment his hasidim thought they saw his soul separate from his body. Hesitating to ask what the nature of this laughter was, out of respect for their master, they could not observe any cause to have brought it about.

Their rebbe continued to sit at the table for some time after the meal, as it was his customary way to extend pursuit of the holy blessings. Then he laughed a second time. After a while, the Besh't laughed a third time. Now, this was a true wonderment to the hasidim, for they had never seen such a thing in their master and teacher.

The Besh't was accustomed to smoke his tobacco pipe after the departure of the Shabbos Queen and the recitation of the havdalah benediction signifying the separation between the holy and the mundane. Every week, it was the habit of Rabbi Ze'ev at that hour to inquire of the Besh't the meaning of all that had transpired on the Sabbath. Since of course nothing was haphazard in Creation. The hasidim hoped that perhaps this evening Rabbi Ze'ev would ask their teacher to explain the meaning of his three laughs?

And so it was that Rabbi Ze'ev Kizes came to the chamber of the Besh't and asked,

- Will our master explain the laughter which Rabbenu laughed at the Shabbos eve table?

Then the Besh't emerged from his chamber and addressed all the hasidim,

- I will show you the substance of the matter which caused me to laugh.

The rebbe asked that the horses be harnessed to his wagon. And this too was the Besh't's way, to sojourn out into the countryside after restrictions of the holy day. The rebbe instructed that each hasid take everyday clothing, for surely they would not return that evening, and all sat themselves in the wagon to accompany the Besh't. They rode all that night, knowing not from where and to where.

At the morning's light, they arrived at a large city under G-d by the name of Kojznitz. The Besh't and his party took up hostel with the parnassim of that city who were happily waiting to welcome them, since word of the Besh't visit had reached their ears. And all the Jews of Kojznitz came out to greet this shining zaddik.

After the morning shacharit prayers, the Besh't inquired about Reb' Shabtai the book-binder. The Kojznitz Jewish notables asked,

- What can that old man be to you? For he is one of the most humble men of our city. It is true that he is an honest man, but very simple and without Torah learning.

The Besh't replied,

- No matter. It is my wish that we go to him.

And so it was.

They came to their destination, and the Besh't said to Reb' Shabtai,

- Call your wife, that she might speak with us here.

Then the Besh't asked the old couple,

- Tell us what you both were about on the previous Shabbat eve, but speak the truth as it was. Have no fear of those gathered here.

The people of Kojznitz and the hasidim of the Besh't gave attentive ear to hear what the old people might say. All drew close to see what would be the outcome of this matter.

Reb' Shabtai spoke,

- With your permission, I will not deny all that has befallen me, and if I have sinned, the rebbe will help me to repair . . .

- I have always supported myself from my craft of book-binding, and as long as my strength held true, I made a good living from my skill. And, I was a bit well off. During all those years it was my custom to purchase all the Shabbos needs: flour, fish and meat, wine and candles for the blessing and all other necessities on Thursday of that Sabbath week. The next day, at the noon hour of Sabbath eve, I would cease my labors and work no more that day. I went to the bet-knesset, that I might prepare my soul, and to there recite King Solomon's Song of Songs and the Shabbos tikkun liturgy. There I would stay, in the synagogue, until all the usual prayers were recited. Only then would I return home. And this was my custom since the days of my youth.

- Now I am old and the wheel has turned against me. I no longer have the strength to support myself from my labors as before. Because of this, I live my life in poverty and sorrow. I am no longer able to purchase all our Shabbos needs on the fifth day of the week, as was my custom. . . But, no matter what befalls me, I never relinquish the mitzvah of going to bet-knesset at the noon hour of the Sabbath eve.

- And so it happened that on this last holy Shabbat eve, the noon hour had arrived and still I had not one kopek for our needs. I had not even brought my wife flour for the challah bread. When I saw that there was no indication and

Lighting Sabbath Candles – I. Snowman

no source from which to furnish our holy day, and since never in all my life did I have need to turn to others for help, I found no readiness in me now to ask charity from some benefactor, or to beg at the doors of others . I decided that it was better to suffer on the Sabbath, rather than to accept a gift from a flesh and blood man.*

- However, I was greatly concerned lest my wife not have the resolve to refrain from seeking out help from our neighbors – a candle to light or a challah bread, fish or meat. For this reason, I asked that she not accept a gift from our neighbors, though they might seek her out and press her to do so. For the children of Israel are compassionate, and if our people see that one has not the means to prepare Sabbath, they urge you to accept from their hands.

- She promised that she would not accept our neighbors charity, and we shook hands in agreement. Fasting for lack of food, I explained to my wife that I wished to hurry to bet-knesset before the noon hour, "At the bet-knesset, the people will approach me and ask, 'Why is a Shabbat candle not burning in your window?' And what can I say to them? Therefore, after prayers I will wait until all the people have gone. Only then will I come home. In this way, we will accept all the trials and suffering decreed upon us from the Almighty with love."

- I went to the synagogue, and my wife cleaned the house, honoring it for Shabbos as best she could . . . Now, what happened was that she found two old gloves which had been lost to us for several years, and these gloves were fashioned with silver and gold buttons as had been the custom of our brethren Israel. She hurried to the silversmith to sell the buttons and the money was sufficient for all our Shabbat needs. There was even food remaining for the weekdays. It being too late to prepare dough, she purchased the challah breads and meat and fish for the Shabbos table. And since she knew that I would delay at the synagogue until after twilight, she herself purchased two large Shabbat candles, that they might alight the honor of the sacred Shekninah.

- Evening fell, and when all the people had departed the bet-knesset, I also left there. From afar I saw a lit candle in our window and said in my heart, "Here we have it, my wife did not have the strength of will to prevent herself from accepting a gift from flesh and blood man." With this thought, I arrived to my house. However, when I saw the table set with challah, fish and wine for kiddush.

I thought, "If I scold her, I will spoil the joy. For this reason, I delayed my comment and greeted her with, "-Shabbos Shalom". I blessed the wine and tasted of the fish. Only then did I mention, in a gentle way, "It seems that you are not able to accept the bad times." And what did she say?

"Surely you remember the gloves with silver and gold buttons which had been lost to us all this time?" "Yes, yes, I do remember," I replied. "Well, I found them today as I was cleaning. . . And in exchange for the buttons I purchased all the needs of the Sabbath."

- When I heard her words, tears of joy poured from my eyes, and I thanked the Blessed Benefactor of the Universe that He had sent me down His own charity to permit me to honor the Shabbos. Unable to cease my rejoicing, I took my wife by the hand and led her in an ecstasy of dance for an hour or more. And after I sat to taste a bit of soup, I rose to dance a second time. . . Then again I danced after I ate the compote, and saw that my Shabbos table was as laden as that of a king.

- I danced three times together with my wife on that evening, for I was not able to contain the exceptional joy within me. The blessed Almighty had considered me deserving. He had permitted me to pleasure in the Shabbos with challot and wine, with meat and fish, and all this by means of His open and generous hand, the Holy Blessed be

His Name. And not by means of the gift of flesh and blood man.

When the book-binder had finished his tale, the Besh't addressed his hasidim,

- Believe me, all the celestial household laughed and danced together with Reb' Shabtai of Kojznitz and his wife. That is when I, too, laughed. And I laughed three times for each time that they danced.

The Besh't then asked that the wife of Shabtai approach, and said to her,

- What do you prefer? To live out the remainder of your days in honor and wealth, or to birth a son who will comfort you in your old age?

She replied that she and Reb' Shabtai, who was already seventy years old, were childless. Therefore, she asked for a son to warm their elder years.

And the Besh't blessed the old couple thus,

- If so, I have glad tidings. Next year at this season I will return to thee, for at that time thee shall birth a son and name him Israel, as my name is Israel. This splendid son will light up the next world for you, and his good deeds add to the scale of your virtues after you have passed on to the world of truth . . . Therefore, next year at this season, call for me to return to thee. Then shall I hold the child when he is circumcised; at his brit mila I shall be sandak.

And so it was.

On the next year, the woman gave birth to a son who was to become the Rabbi Maggid Israel of Kojznitz, the author of "Avodat Yisrael" and "Tehilot Yisrael". He was a great zaddik and a very modest and holy man. Who can count the thousandfold ways in which he was a hasid? May his virtues protect and be our guardian always.

* The Jew is instructed to strictly avoid suffering or unhappiness on the Sabbath. For instance, the seven day period of mourning is suspended during the interval between Friday evening and the close of the Sabbath.

Lest a Pauper
Become a Thief

There came before the Maggid Rabbi Israel of Kojznitz, of sainted memory, a certain excellent hasid, who was a true sage and highly learned in Torah. Genuinely depressed in a poverty which his wisdom could not resolve, he had come to consult with the Maggid, and to ask in what way he could support his household.

The Maggid said to him,

- I can see that your mazal does not indicate success in any merchant trade. Indeed, there is only occupation at which you can achieve wealth.

- Your wisdom is as the Holy Book, Kevod Torahto. Therefore, I respectfully ask that you reveal it to me.

- What use to tell you of this thing? For I well know that you will have no wish for it at all.

- Surely, by reason of my great poverty I cannot refuse.

After some thought, the Maggid said,

- Know this. You have a superior mazal in the affairs of thievery.

Startled into amazement and in a fright, the hasid called out,

- How can I seek such a profession? It is against the will of the Blessed be His Name!

- It is just as I said — you will not want to work at this profession. But I observe that you have no success at any other occupation except that of stealing, and I can tell you that out of thievery fortune will emerge and increase most wonderfully.

The hasid returned to his home, spirits very low. In succeeding days the situation went from bad to worse, until a time that he and his wife and children had not eaten bread for several days, and he wept to watch their souls expiring. Thereupon, he began to ponder this unusual issue in his mind. With the customary logic of a Torah scholar, he weighed and considered the approaches to this severe conflict in the following manner,

- The matter has become one of life or death. To save an endangered life takes precedence even over the holiness of the Sabbath. Now, since thievery is a less severe crime than profaning of the Sabbath, why does saving a life not take precedence over the prohibition to steal?

Very unhappy at his conclusion, he nevertheless became committed to the decision to steal for his family. Thus, one night he proceeded to dig under the entrance of a certain shop where he stole stole only one gold coin. With this he purchased bread and vegetables to sustain himself and his household. And all the while, in his mind was the intention to return this gold coin to the shop's owner when the Almighty would expand his borders and he would be granted respite from his poverty.

The next morning, when the shopkeeper arrived and discovered that the shop had been broken into, he raised a shout,

- Aya! I have been made poor!

But when he entered the shop, he saw that all his merchandise was intact, he very much wondered at this.

Opening the cashbox, he saw that only one gold coin was missing, although the chest was filled with many such coins.

And all the town wondered at this strange thief.

The hasid supported his family for several days with this coin, on very narrow rations. What mattered was that he and his family would not die of starvation. Until a day came that there was not one remaining scrap of bread.

Again, he went to steal, and it was as the first time. He entered a locked shop, took only one gold coin, and bought food for his household. In this way, he robbed several more shops, until the matter had become an exceptional puzzle for the whole town. For what kind of thief was this – one who breaks in to steal one gold coin! The residents of the town posted watchmen at the shops to catch the thief, with no success. The hasid was not to be discovered. It was as the Rabbi Maggid, of blessed memory, had told him: in the profession of stealing he had a superior mazal. Thus did the matter take its course. The townspeople tried to catch the thief, but could not.

Now, rumor of this tale reached the manor prince of that town who wondered exceedingly at it, for how could so many guards be unable to catch one thief. And how was it that they never saw the thief? So the manor prince announced to the townspeople,

- I myself will capture him.

Night after night, the manor prince had paced between the shops and watched to catch the thief, without success, for during that interval the hasid had some remaining morsels to feed his family and refrained from stealing. Until the day when their bread was finished, and on that night, as he had become accustomed, he emerged from his house and went to steal one gold coin.

On this night, although the watchmen kept their eyes on each and every shop, they did not know that one shop was broken into and one gold coin stolen. But the manor prince, who was disguised in peasant clothing so that he would not be recognized, watched the hasid break into the shop, open the money box and take one gold coin.

He grabbed hold of him, calling out,

- You are the thief of the gold coins! I will take you to the prince of this town and there we will hear what judgment he lays upon you.

The hasid pleaded that the man leave him be,

- O' my prince, I will be immensely shamed, for I am considered one of the learned Jews of this town. You can see that your servant is not, G-d forbid, a notorious kind of thief. I only take one gold coin from each shop, although I could have taken all the merchandise. The truth is I do not want to steal at all, and only out of great poverty must I do this. When the Blessed G-d extends my borders, and with His help, I will return all these gold coins in full.

But the man who was in truth the manor prince held on tightly,

- You will not escape from me until I hand you over to the prince. He will do with you what he decides.

The hasid began to weep copious tears, to beg and plead exceedingly. At which the disguised prince said,

- Look here, I can see that your luck is good in affairs of thievery. Therefore, if you do my will, I will allow you to go free. The matter is such. A great sum of money arrived today to the prince's manor from the cities of his province and the chest filled with money has been secreted under the prince's bed. The royal chamber has a small window through which you will enter, and when you bring to me this chest filled with great treasure, we share it between us.

Hearing this, the hasid began to weep more bitterly. His soul was sickened, and he again pleaded with the man who would thus ensnare him,

- Sir, you can see that I am not a thief, G-d forbid, for I only take one gold coin.

Drawing – H. Struck

But the disguised prince would not hear of it,

- If you persist, I hand you over immediately to the manor prince and he will do with you what he will.

The hasid could see that there was no way to avoid this trouble. So, he followed his captor to the home of the manor prince, and there was shown the window of the room wherein lay the money chest. Clambering up in sight of the disguised prince, after a short time the hasid descended, saying to the man masquerading as his accomplice,

- Praise to the Almighty who has saved me from this act of thievery!

Surprised, the manor prince asked,

- And why is this?

The hasid explained,

- Because I have just heard two servents of the manor prince conspiring, and one said to his mate, "Guard this deathly poison carefully. In the morning we will put it to good use in the prince's tea so as to kill him and steal his treasure of money. For there is no other man in the world who knows what this chest contains."

The hasid continued,

- In my opinion, we should go directly to the prince of the manor to prevent him, G-d forbid, from drinking the poisoned tea in the morning. Then surely he will award us a considerable prize.

When the prince heard this, an exceeding fright fell upon him, and he said,

- Go, return now to your house, and only leave me with the hat which you wear.

The hasid happily gave over his hat to the disguised prince. Walking quickly home, he rejoiced that he had been saved both from this great act of thievery and from the hands of his captor.

For, in truth, the prince had plotted to catch the hasid out in a great robbery so as to inflict a more severe justice upon him.

The manor prince returned to his home and to his own costume. He lay down in his bed, but he could not sleep for his heart clamored and clanged like the great town bell. With the light of morning, he instructed his two servants to bring in his morning cup of tea. They entered, placing the cup ot tea directly into his hand to ensure that the prince might drink of it swiftly. But when they handed him the glass, he said to one,

- Drink you first of this glass.

Under no circumstances would the man drink, and also the second servant would not drink. Then the manor prince know for certain that the hasid had not lied, and he gave the tea to the dog who fell immediately dead to the ground.

The manor prince sentenced these two servants to death by cruel and unusual means. He then called for the Jewish notables of the town to come to the manor. Showing them the hasid's hat, he asked,

- Do you know to whom this hat belongs?

- Yes, we know the man.

Then he said to them,

- The owner of this hat is the man who has stolen the gold coins!

Amazed, they leaped up,

- Your excellency, this is an impossible thing. The owner of this hat is an exceeding scholar and a noble man among the Jews!

- Call for him, that he might appear before me, immediately.

Thus, the hasid was summoned to the manor, bearing his broken heart and his shame. There, he saw that his captor had been the prince himself, who now questioned him,

- Do you know to whom this hat belongs?

- Sir, it is mine.

But the prince addressed him gently,

- My friend, the Jewish notables of the town have already told me of your excellence and that you would engage in stealing gold coins is a great wonder in my eyes, for I can see that you are as far from such matters as one can be. But I can sense that the sequence of these events have been directed by the Almighty, so as to save me from cruel murder.

Then the prince told his side of the tale, and of his plot to capture the hasid in a great crime.

- But now, it is just and it is fair that the great chest of money should be yours, since you have saved me from death. Let us share it half and half as we agreed when we were comrade thieves.

The hasid gratefully accepted half this great fortune as his own. And his first action was to return each gold coin to the shop from whence it came.

It was said of this hasid that he lived the remaining days of his life in exceptional wealth, and he always trusted in the Almighty with pious faith. He performed many mitzvot and distributed considerable monies to all those who learned Torah, and especially to the most meritorious Torah scholars and the poor and needy.

A Letter in Season and Time

This is a true story of a particular journey which the Ba'al Shem Tov and his disciple hasidim undertook to the Jewish communities of the land. In one town the Besh't and his party were always hosted by a certain Jewish magnate who loved to be kind at all times and benevolant at a moment's notice. The doors to this man's home were open wide, that all might come and go freely. As in the past, wealthy gevir now welcomed the Besh't with great respect, as was due him, and arranged for a great banquet to honor the zaddik and his hasidim.

When the visit was over and before the Ba'al Shem, of blessed memory, parted to go on his way, he said to his host,

- Tell me your need and I will fill it.

- Glory to the Blessed G-d, the Almighty has looked with favor upon me and I have nothing I need ask of kedosho.

Then the Besh't said to him,

- If so, I will ask a small favor of you, and do not refuse me.

- With my whole being and my might, I am servant of your

excellence. Any matter you command, I will do. Forbid that I might leave you empty-handed.

The rebbe sat down at the table and composed a letter which he signed with his own signature and hand. On the envelope he noted, "For the new parnassim of the city of Brad, the Rabbis . . . " and here he wrote in their names.

Giving the letter over to his host, he explained,

- It is my wish that you carry this letter with your own hand to the city of Brad, and deliver it to the parnassim whose names I have written here.

The householder took the letter from the sainted rebbe and put it for safekeeping into the pocket of his coat,

- Yes, yes, I will do as your excellence has asked.

Then the Besh't said,

- Now it is my wish to be on my way. Please accompany me to the wagon.

At the stable, the host hurried to take hold of the horse's reins in order to saddle them himself. But when he bent over the stable box, the letter slipped out of his coat pocket and fell into the box. And the gevir knew not of it. Harnessing the horses, he accompanied the Besh't and his party a short distance along their way. Then he returned to his house and the matter of the letter was completely forgotten.

And so it was that many days passed and time came that the holy ark was secreted away; the Besh't was taken to be with the Almighty.

At about that time, the good fortune of the wealthy magnate turned against him. He was brought low and lost all his property. Now an impoverished man, he was forced to sell all his possessions in order to support his household. And he continued to care for the paupers who sat around his table, as was his exemplary custom. This state of affairs continued for many days, until it was seventeen years after the time that the Besh't, of sacred memory, had left this world.

The day came that this householder went to the stable box, to see if perhaps there was something there to sell so as to keep his soul alive. He removed its contents and there on the bottom of the box lay the letter from the holy vessel, the Ba'al Shem Tov, of blessed memory. Wondering greatly at seeing it, his heart fell in his bosom when he looked more closely and recognized the handwriting of the Besh't,

- O' Woe! Now I know from what place my unfortunate mazal has fallen upon me, for what reason and why my success deserted me.

But still, he did not make so bold as to dare open the letter and read what had been written there. He decided in his heart that he must carry the letter to the city of Brad. Perhaps there he would find the parnassim whose names were written on the envelope and they could still have some good use of it.

Immediately, he took himself from his town and set out on the lengthy and difficult walk to the city of Brad. Once there, he asked for lodging at the beit-midrash, as was the custom of the poor. Then he began to search out these parnassim that had served the community of Brad twenty years ago.

- One old man to whom he related the incident of the letter, said,

- I clearly remember that from the day that I grew into manhood until this time, there never have been two parnassim serving the city of Brad with names such as appear on this envelope.

The man who has been the Besht's host asked a second and a third person, but all answered as did the first. As he stood in the street asking questions of the passersby, one man approached him, and declared,

- Today there is a ballot in the committee building to elect new parnassim. Perhaps the men with these names will be

Scribe – L. Reis

elected, the ones whom you search for!

The Jews standing about there laughed mirthfully at this joke. As they spoke, two youths entered the beit-midrash calling out in a jolly way,

- Mazal tov to the community, the two Rabbi's, so-and-so have been elected by ballot to be the new parnassim. All the people now accompany them to the committee house to install them on their seat of office.

The hasid asked the names of the new parnassim and, lo, these were the very names written by the Besh't on the envelope which he held in his hand.

At the community house, he approached the new parnassim, two young men about twenty or twenty five,

- Blessed ones who serve the Almighty, here is a letter which the holy Besh't has sent to you!

The new parnassim looked at him, mouths overcome with laughter and saying,

- From where have you come, you fool, to bring us a letter from the holy Besh't who has gone from this world seventeen years now?

The hasid replied and told them with a grieved and humbled spirit,

- I come from a certain village and in my eyes as well it is a wonder. But this is how the matter came about.

Then he related all that had befallen him, saying,

- Now open this letter and see what is written there. Perhaps it can bring some good. I myself was feared to open it. I can see now that this thing is one of the wonders which the Creator of the Universe brings about.

The new parnassim accepted the letter and opened it. Its contents were as follows:

"To Rabbis so-and-so, the new parnassim of the Jewish community of Brad. Here is one man who submits my letter to you, and he appeals to your good offices. Make every effort to be magnanimous, for he is a worthy and decent man who has now fallen into poverty. In a previous time he lived in great wealth, but the days have turned upon him and he stumbles about in the world, come low from all his property. Therefore, make your effort to serve him well. I, Rabbi Ba'al Shem Tov ask this of you."

And this wonderful letter continued,

"If you do not believe that it is truly I who have sent this letter to you, I will give you a clear sign. Very soon messengers will come to inform you of a joyful event. Both your wives are presently with child. Now, the wife of so and so will give birth to a fine son and the wife of so and so will give birth to a healthy daughter. This will be your sign that it is I, the Ba'al Shem, who writes this letter. I have done all this that you might look out for this good man and do your best for him.

"Signed . . . 'Rabbi Israel Ba'al Shem Tov'."

Before they could finish reading the letter, here came the harbingers of good news to inform them that their wives had just given birth. And it was just as it had been written in the letter!

All the city was in tumult and turmoil, the people amazed at the great wisdom of our meritous teacher and master, the Besh't of sainted memory.

This hasid was soon again a wealthy man, as all that town offered him their best. While the new parnassim added their blessings for his good health, praying with all their heart and soul that he would know only good fortune until the end of his days.

Choose a Rabbi to Advise You

O nce a destitute man of injured spirit came before the Ba'al Shem Tov to ask that the rebbe perform a wondrous act to save him. The Ba'al Shem Tov advised that the poor man go to a certain bridge; under it he would discover a cache of gold. Thus, he would be delivered from his poverty. The man took himself to that bridge; he searched and searched, but found no gold.

Walking along the road, he came across an acquaintance, a destitute tailor, a wretched pauper like himself – would that the Almighty rescue them both – who asked him,

- For what and why has your face fallen thus, and what is your wish?

He related what the Ba'al Shem Tov had instructed him, saying,

- For naught did I labor, for I have found naught.

His friend the tailor replied,

- My case is similar. For the Besh't also advised me to enter a certain house and there behind the oven I would find a fortune. However, I did not do so, not having the courage in my soul to dig secretly in the house of another man.

The first man listened to his acquaintance with a

throbbing heart, for the house described and that very oven were his own house and his oven. He said in his soul, "Since I am the one who lives in that house, I will go there and search behind my oven. Perhaps I will find the secreted fortune.

This he did and found a fortune in gold coins.

Meanwhile the poor tailor also thought his thoughts, "-Here I am, at this very bridge. Why should I mind to look about a bit? Perhaps the words of my friend, as instructed by the Ba'al Shem Tov, are true and real and I will find my fortune.

So that one searched as well. And truly found the cache of gold and silver coins which the Besh't had spoken of. He too was a wealthy man.

Now each man became troubled in his heart, and each thought,

- It was because of my friend that I found the cache of gold. Therefore how can I observe him living in poverty. How can I stay silent when I found his fortune?

So each decided to bring the other a share, a fine knot of money, that his friend's situation might be improved; and this is what they did.

Along the way, they met. After the tales were happily told, they wondered what should be done with the knots of money intended by each for his comrade. It was decided that, since one had a son and the other a daughter, their children would be matched for marriage, and the fine knot sacks filled with gold and silver coins serve as their children's dowry.

Rabbi Zevi Hirsch of Kamenka was accustomed to say that this true tale should always be related after the Shabbat at the festive melave malka meal, since the telling is a treasured remedy for good livelihood.

And the Rabbi also would say,

- Every man and woman in Israel is ready for a superb

rescue from the Almighty, and prepared to find the hidden treasure intended especially for each one. But this deliverance depends on mutual help and love.

In this way the Almighty assists us, that we may honor His name.

Chasid Dancing – Tully Filmus

Reincarnation of the Soul

T his is a story that took place in the town of Medzibezh, where resided the Ba'al Shem Tov. There was one talmid hahkam in this town, a G-d-fearing man, who sat and learned Torah day and night. This Torah scholar was impoverished, and kept his soul alive only with the help of compassionate Jews who offered occasional charity with which he fed himself and his family.

His wife, a G-d-fearing woman who never sorrowed her husband the Torah scholar, so as not to cause him to neglect his learning. She satisfied herself with what the blessed Lord brought to her in His benefaction.

The days passed, and their sons and daughters were soon grown and had come of marriage age. Then his modest wife came to him and said,

- It is true that we trust in the blessed Almighty, in His great pity He maintains us. But what of our sons and daughters, who are now grown and we must marry them off? For we have no money or any object of value at hand. Please, my husband, propose your solution.

The Torah scholar said to her,

- And what shall I do? The Almighty has not as yet

dispatched good fortune from the sanctity of His justice to our family.

Now, his goodly wife had a strong preference for the zaddikim and was an especially firm believer in the Zaddik Rabbi Yisrael Ba'al Shem Tov, the first hasid of that generation, who resided in their town. Already renowned for the mystical wonders he had performed, many had been rescued through his prayers. As the Sages say, what a zaddik decrees, the Holy One Blessed Be His Name carries out.

So the woman approached her husband,

- My husband, hearken to me. It is true that you have not been accustomed to adhere to the zaddik hasidim and to join their court, but please observe and notice that many Torah observant men and women who are without blemish have been rescued by the prayers and effort of the zaddik. For what the Besh't decrees comes about. Perhaps you also can be helped by him. Only agree and incline yourself in his direction. Therefore, I ask that you go to him and ask that he pray for us. And whatever he instructs you to do – obey.

The Torah scholar agreed to see the Ba'al Shem Tov and when he stood before him, he unburdened himself of all the matters weighing heavy on his heart.

The Besh't's response was that he must travel to the city of Kazimerz and there ask after a certain Jew, the son of so-and-so, who was employed at a particular craft. The talmud hahkam must search for this man until he found him, for only thus would he find release from his misery.

The Torah scholar took upon himself the travails of the road, and the soles of his shoes became worn walking from city to town until he came to Kazimerz, as instructed him by the man of G-d. The custom of that place was that when a poor and wretched stranger would come among them, he would be hosted at the travelers' hostel there to rest from the rigors of the road. At the hostel which was crowded with many people, the Torah scholar asked after the man whom the Ba'al Shem Tov had instructed him to find. And all replied that they did not know if there was such a man of such a father in the entire city. For no one knew these names.

The Torah scholar sighed deeply, that he should have wearied himself on the road for naught. His feet had trod a distance of sixty parasangs to find the wanted man.   •

He then went to the bet-midrash to inquire, and too here the man's name, the name of his father and his particular craft, as well as other signs which were given to him by the Besh't were unknown to all. Told and retold throughout the city until the Jews all knew that a Torah scholar searched for such and such a person; and only then did the elders of the town come to him, asking,

- What is this? Why do you ask for that evil man who has these sixty years past been dead and gone from the world?

Then they related the habits of that deceased man and the evil of his wanton and capricious behavior. For he did not permit even one transgression, pity be to him, to pass him by without indulging in it. They exclaimed,

- A description of the many monstrous details cannot pass over the threshold of a decent man's lips!

The Torah scholar did not reveal to them the secrets of his heart and chose to speak to several other elders. They too censured this man for whom he searched. Then, he knew for certain that this person had been most evil, and there was no one like him.

The Torah scholar carried himself home, there to sit in a misery of soul that allowed entry to no ray of light. Weary from the great effort of his travels and the outcome, he felt he had no strength to bear his misery. After a short time he went to the Ba'al Shem Tov to learn from him the root of the matter and hear the opinion of the rebbe regarding his journey.

When he came before the Besh't, he related of his travels,

- I came to the city where our excellent teacher sent me. There I learned that a Jewish artisen of the name given to me, whose father's name was such-and-such, is dead and gone from the world for sixty years now. But the worst of it is, that this man was most evil.

The talmid hahkam told the Besh't all the terrible things the elders had related, for the man he was sent to seek out had been a transgressor who did not allow one wickedness to go undone.

The Besh't heard him out and after a while said,

- You are a Torah scholar and an observant Jew. Doubtless and with true faith you believe in transmigration of the soul as declared in the kabbalah. Therefore, know this. Sixty years ago your own soul occupied the body of that man who did not permit one transgression to go undone. In a previous life you were that wicked man!

- Now, in your present life your soul has been given the opportunity to return and cleanse itself of those prior blemishes. You received the greatest gift man can hope for; can you ask for more than this? Do you dare to also ask for the delicacies and pleasures of corporeal man?

When the Torah scholar heard the words of the Ba'al Shem Tov, he became very terrified. Thereupon, he asked the Besh't to compile a tikkun for him, that he might correct and free himself of all the sins of his previous existence, once and for all.

For the rest of his days, this talmud hahkam continued to bind his soul to Torah and prayer, and to study with great diligence and constancy in conditions of dire poverty. In years thereafter, he became one of the most brilliant students of the Ba'al Shem Tov. May his virtues in the Almighty protect us all.

Marital Harmony

Before his name was revealed in Israel and prior to his becoming renowned at the gates, Rabbi Jechiel Michael, the Maggid of Zloczow, resided in the city of Yampol which was near to Medzibezh, where dwelled Rabbi Israel Ba'al Shem Tov.

One of the devotees of the Besh't, a cattle merchant, was accustomed to visit the rebbe before each journey to the Yampol fair, and pass the Sabbath in that modest court.

Once, as he bid the merchant "safe journey", the Ba'al Shem Tov also said,

- When you arrive in Yampol, greet Rabbi Michael in my name.

In Yampol, the merchant troubled long to search out the one whom the Besh't called "Rabbi Michael", but to no avail. Finally he entered the bet-midrash, and even the familiars who frequented the Torah study hall daily could only say,

- Rabbi Michael? No, we have no knowledge of such a rabbi.

As he was about to leave, one of the men called over,

- There is one man in our city by the name Michael, but he certainly is not entitled "Rabbi". The children call him "the mad one," and only they pay him any mind. So, what is your interest in a man whose habit when he prays is to strike his head against the wall until blood pours freely?

- I wish to speak to him.

- This is not an easy matter. He sits at home over his books of Torah, so diligent that it is impossible to interrupt him. Only when one comes to whisper in his ear, "I want to eat!" does he pick himself up and run out into the street to seek out food for his guest; acting according to the instruction that the mitzvah of hospitality precedes even that of Torah learning. And, that is the only occasion you can succeed in addressing him.

The cattle merchant asked the way to the the mad one's dwelling, and arriving at the door of a shabby house where a child sat clad in rags, he permitted himself entry. Rabbi Michael sat bent over an open volume of the kaballah, and did not lift his eyes when the visitor entered.

The merchant approached him and whispered,

- I want to eat!

Immediately, Rabbi Michael rose and looked about the room. He searched the closets, but they all were empty of food. Taking down one of his books from the bookshelf, he ran out. Handing it to the grocer as security, he brought back some bread and herring for his hungry guest.

After he ate, the merchant said,

- The Ba'al Shem Tov asked me to inquire after your health.

Rabbi Michael bent his head and was silent.

After a while, the merchant said,

- Rabbi Michael, I see in you a holy man. Therefore, you have only to pray for wealth and surely you will have it. Why do you live in such poverty?

Thereupon Rabbi Michael spoke, and related this parable,

- There was a king who held a wedding feast for his beloved daughter. He invited all the people of his capital city

Putting on Tefillin for the first time

and each citizen was sent a printed invitation and a detailed menu of the feast.

- Suddenly, the princess fell ill. The doctors rushed to her, but after several hours she was dead. A pall and gloom took hold of all the guests who had come to celebrate a wedding which had ended in tragedy. The people fell silent and slowly each took his leave, for the city mourned the beautiful and kind princess who had been taken from them in the prime of her youth.

- Except for one man who remained seated in his place, holding the festive menu in his hand. He called to the servants and, without shame, asked that all the foods listed there be brought to his table. They served him and he smacked his lips over every tasty morsel.

Rabbi Yechiel Michael continued,

- Shall I behave as this man? For the Shekhinah, the Divine Presence which is the very soul of Israel is in exile !

This is why Rabbi Yechiel Michael the Maggid of Zloczow chose to remain a humble pauper all the days of his life.

Another tale of the Maggid of Zloczow.

One year, prior to the eve of the Sukkoth festival, Rabbi Michael did not have money to purchase an etrog citron over which to make the blessing of the Four Species. That year the harvest had been bad and the citron was priced very dear. Only the wealthy patrician of the town had enough money to purchase a splendid and perfect etrog.

Now Rabbi Yechiel Michaeli's tefillin, which he had inherited from his father, were the handwork of a well-known and devout Torah scribe. He took them in hand and gave thought to the problem to himself, "One is permitted to pray with borrowed tefillin, but one is not permitted to recite the Four Species blessing over a borrowed etrog, of which it is said, "And you will take to yourself . . . a fruit of the citrus tree." For the Sages interpret this sentence to mean, "An etrog belonging to you."

So Rabbi Michael came to the gevir and said,

- I offer you my tefillin in exchange for your etrog.

The gevir agreed and each was happy and satisfied with the transaction. Rabbi Michael had a splendid etrog, while the gevir had obtained a set of tefillin, the scrolls of which were written by a famous and devout scribe, and upon which the zaddik Rabbi Yechiel Michael had invested his virtue.

Rabbi Yechiel Michael returned home with the etrog in his hand, anxious to share the happiness of this great fortune which had befallen him with his wife. However, instead of being joyous with him, his soul-mate became very angry, and she shouted,

- All the people say that you are a great zaddik. But what kind of zaddik is it who would not sell his tefillin to feed a hungry family, but sells tefillin so as to glorify himself with a fine etrog? . . You are hard-hearted and cruel.

At this, she threw the etrog on the ground in anger and its fine stem, which is necessary to its kosher status, was broken off.

Then, seeing what she had done, she broke into tears

However, her husband, the zaddik Rabbi Michael, did not become angry but comforted her instead,

- Do not let it worry you. I am not angry, G-d forbid, for you did this out of a broken heart, not an evil heart.

Then Rabbi Yechiel Michael raised his eyes to the Almighty, and sighed,

- O' Master of the Universe, I have no tefillin now, and I have no etrog. Shall I also heed the weak inclination of my flesh to inflame the anger which instigates man against his wife and is sure to ruin the peace of my home, God forbid!

THE GATES OF
CHARITY
AND COMPASSION

The Wheel Turns

tale of the son of Rabbi Michaeli of Lublin. Once he was traveling from there to the city of Levov. The Jewish personages of the city came out to welcome him, and among them was a certain very wealthy man. The Rabbi scrutinized the countenance of this man, then addressed him,

- I have something to relate to you.

- Speak sir.

And the Rabbi began, - Pay heed and listen to this tale . . .

- There were two brothers who lived in the same city, one wealthy and the other poor. For years, the wealthy brother gave the poor brother enough to support himself. One day the wealthy man said in his heart, "My brother is a man of intelligence and can be relied on. It is only lack of money which afflicts him, since he has no ma'ot with which to initiate and succeed in business dealings. Penury has forced him to be locked all his days in need."

- Consulting with his beloved friends and familiars who advised him wholeheartedly to extend a loan of one thousand gold coins to the unfortunate brother, he called upon him and said, "My brother, here are one thousand gold coins. Purchase merchandise with a generous hand. Perhaps the Almighty will favor you and 'He will lift the needy out of the dust'. Would that you now increase and become your own man. Then you will can return this money to me."

- So saying, he gave this money to his poor brother who accepted it joyfully and blessed him, "My brother, you have given me life. May your earnings be doubled from the Almighty above us." Returning in good cheer to his home, he began business affairs, soon succeeded and became a very wealthy man.

- And so it goes, the wheel turned. The wealthy brother descended from his prosperity and was reduced from his property. The ears of all rang with the unhappy tidings, for the man was now a total pauper. His wise advisers and those who loved him said to him, with simple and direct wisdom, "Your brother owes you one thousand ma'ot. This is the very sum which you lent to him in the days when he was a lowly pauper. Go to him and take back the money which is yours. Then you can build yourself up again with investments."

- Their words rang true and he went to see his brother. When he came there, his brother did not greet him or respond when spoken to, behaving as though he were deaf. After this, every day the once wealthy brother would go to his brother's home to weep and implore. But the man did not attend to these pleas. By this time, the family of the once wealthy brother was enfolded in extreme poverty and hunger, and were truly destitute.

- His soul in extreme distress and sickening, the wretched man approached his brother one last time. Again weeping, now he begged only for some small morsel of bread, "Save me my brother; for even the bread has gone from our plates and we have no way to keep our unfortunate souls alive. " But this last time as well the now wealthy brother did not heed his brother who had been brought so low. He was silent and, at that, the pauper's breath left his body together with the words of his mouth, and he died in severe humiliation.

90

- The now wealthy brother did not live long after his pauper brother died. He passed on and when he arrived at the celestial court, he was judged very harshly, and accused of causing the death of his own brother. The heavenly advocates said to him,

- "Look here, O' evil one. When your brother was wealthy, he had pity and lent you one thousand gold coins. Indeed, you came by all your wealth because of him. Whereas when you saw him descending into his sorrow of soul, you did not have pity. When he pleaded with you, you did not hear him. Therefore, his blood is on your hands."

- At this, the soul of the zaddik, the brother who had been wealthy and died a pauper, showed himself to the heavenly court and began to plead leniency for his brother. His soul declared forgiveness for the one thousand gold coins which had not been returned to him and for the suffering which he had endured on earth during his lifetime. He did this so that his brother should not be punished by reason of his own suffering.

- Thereupon, a verdict was issued from the heavenly court that the brother who died wealthy would return to live again as a wealthy man and the poor zaddik brother would return to live again in penury. The poor brother would be able to redeem his thousand gold coins, for the wealthy brother would repay him by degree all the days of his life. Only then would he be cleansed of his crime and free of his punishment. The poor brother accepted this harsh judgement for the love of his brother.

- And so it was. The wealthy brother was reborn into wealth and honor, in a good and successful hour, and the poor brother was returned to this world to again live out a life of poverty. All the days of his life he did wander from the door of one alms-giver to the door of the next wealthy Jew. And he also came begging to the house of that one who had been his wealthy brother in the previous life.

Travelling to the Rebbe

- He appealed to him thus, "See here sir, the hand of the Almighty has afflicted me with much suffering, and I am poor and in distress. I have nothing with which to keep my soul alive. Pity me and my soul. Three days now I am fasting, for I do not have even a dry crust of bread."

- The wealthy man spoke rudely, "Get away and do not stand in my path, because I will give you nothing."

- At this, this poor man's strength gave out from severe starvation, and he crumpled to the earth at the feet of the wealthy brother. Picking himself up, he returned to his home exceedingly shamed, where he collapsed and died.

All this, the son of the Gaon Rabbi Michaeli, of sainted memory, related to the wealthy gevir who had come to welcome him to the city. Hearing of the cruelty of that wealthy man, the gevir spoke out in a loud voice,

- Listen O' heavenly powers ! Attend to and observe the extreme cruel heart of this wealthy brother!

But the Rabbi addressed him harshly, and with a forceful anger,

- Oh, you traitor! It is you who have been cruel. For where is the pauper who, under the stress of suffering yesterday wept and begged before you as you were descending the fine stairway of your home? That man pleaded for your pity, for a kopek to keep his soul alive, but you did not attend his words and he fell to the ground before you. His pure soul left his body by reason of your cruelty.

- Therefore, know ye that the soul of this man was the very soul of your brother who became a pauper in your previous life. It was he who loaned you the one thousand gold coins which brought about your own wealth. And it was he who pleaded for you before the celestial court and agreed to another life of suffering for your sake. O' woe to you and woe to your soul!

The Rabbi turned his back on him and refused to ever see his face again.

Charity Rescues from the Angel of Death

A true story about a wealthy man whose daughter was very modest, beautiful and charming. Three times did her father give her in marriage to three fine and important men. And each time, may G-d save us, on the wedding night the groom died.

The three-times widow said to her father,

- No longer such a fate, that my husbands die. I will sit here a widow and abandoned until the Almighty who is Merciful grants me His clemency.

So there she sat in her widow's weeds for many days.

Now this wealthy man had a brother in another land who was very poor, and this man had ten sons. Every day he and his oldest son would bring felled trees from the forest to sell in the town. And this was their way to eke out a meagre living for themselves and for their household.

It happened one time that they did not manage to sell their wood and had no money with which to purchase bread. That night they hungered, and the next day went out once more to fell trees, there the father fainted. Unable to bear the sight of his father's suffering and poverty, his son's eyes poured many tears. Raising his eyes to the heavens, he thought and thought. After this, he asked permission from his father to depart to the land of his wealthy uncle.

And so it came about that the eldest son arrived at the house of his father's brother where he was welcomed by his uncle and aunt and their widowed daughter who rejoiced at seeing him. His uncle asked after his mother and father and brothers. He visited with them for seven days and when time was past, the elder son said to his uncle,

- I have one request of you, and please do not send me away empty handed.

- Ask, my son, ask what you will.

- I will not until you say that my request will be so.

So his uncle agreed.

The elder son of his brother said to him,

- What I ask of you is that you give me your widowed daughter for a wife.

His uncle heard this and greatly upset, he replied,

- Know my son that, doubtless in retribution for my own sins, certain unfortunate things have happened to my daughter. I must tell you that her grooms die on their wedding night.

The elder son persisted,

- Nevertheless.

- If your motive is money, it is not necessary that you marry her. For I will give you much money and gold. You are a handsome boy and intelligent, and my advice is that you do not endanger yourself.

- But you have already promised you would fulfill my request.

Seeing how matters were, his uncle accepted. Then he told his family.

Wedding Scene

When his daughter, the widow, heard this she began to weep in the bitterness of her soul, calling out,

- Lord of Creation, let your hand be upon me, and not upon this young man!

On the day when the elder son was to sanctify his betrothed, the bride's father invited the elders of the city to the hupa, and set up a canopy under which the groom would sit.

While everyone was occupied with the wedding preparations, an elderly man, who was in truth Elijah the Prophet, appeared to the groom,

- My son, I will advise you correctly, and do not swerve from my advice. Today when you sit down to the wedding feast, a pauper more poor than any in the world will come to you. Immediately when you see him, rise from your chair and seat him in your own place. Honor him with food and drink and attend to him with all your will and concentration.

Saying this, Elijah left the groom and he saw him no more.

Following the ceremony, as the groom sat at the head of the table of wedding guests, one pauper came there. As soon as the groom saw this pauper, he arose and sat him in his place and he did all that the old man had instructed him to do.

After the feast, when the groom wished to join the bride in her room, the pauper followed behind and said to him,

- My son, I have been dispatched by the Almighty who is in all places and fills Creation. And I am here to take your soul.

The groom pleaded,

- Give me time to be with my bride, one year or one-half year.

The pauper, who was the Angel of Death, said to him,

- I cannot.

- Give me thirty days.

98

- I cannot not even give you one hour, because your time and your hour has come to leave this world.

Then the groom said to him,

- Grant me the time to ask leave of my wife and my uncle who is now my father-in-law.

So the Angel of Death, said to him,

- Since you have been compassionate with me, I agree. But go and return quickly.

He hurried to the room where the bride sat, weeping and praying to the Holy One Be His Name that her husband's fate not be that of her first three husbands. The groom asked his bride to open the door and she hurried to do so, holding his hand to kiss him.

But he said,

- I have come to ask your leave, because my end and my time to go the way of all earthly creatures has come. The Angel of Death has appeared to me. He has come to take my soul.

The bride said to her new husband,

- You will not leave this place. Sit here and I will go to to speak to him where he awaits you.

She did so and found the Angel of Death, to whom she said,

- Are you the messenger who came to take the soul of my husband?

- Yes, I am.

- But is it not written thus in the Torah, "When a man has taken a new wife, he shall not go out to war, neither shall he be charged with any business; but he shall be free at home one year, and shall cheer his wife whom he has taken." The Almighty is truth and His Torah is truth, therefore, will you take the soul of my husband and, G-d forbid, cause the words of Torah to be emptied of their meaning? Now, if you accept my words – well and good. And if not, accompany me to the heavenly court and there let us both be judged by the Almighty Himself.

The Angel of Death heard her out, then said,

- Since your husband has been compassionate with me and even extended me honor, I willingly look upon your request with favor. I go, therefore, directly to the Almighty to relate the matter of which you speak.

The Angel of Death went to ask the Holy One, and in the swiftness of an eye's blink returned. His expression was happy, and he said to the widow,

- Because of the kindness and respect which your husband extended to me and thus to all paupers, the Holy One has has relinquished the judgment and cancelled the decree.

All that night the father and the mother of the bride circled and recircled the house where the groom and the bride were embosomed. And they hearkened joyfully to the happy nuptial sounds. In the morning, the parents of the bride entered the bridal chamber and all celebrated together.

They informed the Jewish community that the decree had been annulled, and everyone gave praise and thanksgiving to the Holy One, Hallowed Be His Name, for this excellent outcome.

And it was as it is written, " Charity rescues from death". Not only strange and unusual death, but from the Angel of Death himself.

Sitting Shiva – Alphonso Levi

THE GATES OF
MITZVAH AND
GOOD DEED

My Heart
is Moved

A tale of Rabbi Moshe Leib of Sasov, of blessed memory. It was the eve of Yom Kippur, that most holy of all days. Sasov's Jews were crowded into the town's synagogues. At the bet knesset of Rabbi Moshe Leib all his hasidim and others who chose to pray in his light awaited the arrival of the zaddik. But still he tarried.

The sun was posed low and about to set, yet he did not appear. The congregation, poised at the threshhold of this important day, began to chant the Kol Nidre prayer. But only when darkness of night had fallen did Rabbi Moshe Leib finally enter the house of worship.

The hasidim asked their rebbe the cause of this delay, a serious and unusual occurence. Thereupon, he laid bare his soul to them,

On his way to Kol Nidre, he heard the sounds of a child crying. Its tears were unabated. Hurrying to the place of that forlorn sound, he found no one there to care for the child which had been left on its own. The mother had gone to synagogue and left her child to tears.

The rebbe's pity was aroused and he lingered to attend

105

the child until it finally fell into a slumber. Only then did the saintly man continue on his way to the synagogue.

Rabbi Moshe Leib then told his hasidim:

- I learned love of my brethren Israel from a simple peasant who at a rustic celebration, his heart content with wine, asked his comrade:

- Do you love me?

And his friend replied,

- My love for you is strong.

Now the peasant asked his comrade,

- How can you say that your love for me is earnest when you know not what I lack? If this love was true you would be quick to see my need!

At this his friend fell silent.

- Thus I was instructed, said Rabbi Moshe Leib of Sasov, as to the true meaning of the term, "love of my brethren Israel".

This is when your heart does truly observe and your soul perceives your fellow-man's needs. You suffer his pain, and his troubles become your own.

The Hunter's Snare Has Been Broken

There was one Jew, a pure hearted and honest hasid who greatly loved to peform the mitzvah of sincerely helping his fellow Israelites. By profession he was a mohel who engaged in the ritual circumcision of boy children and he never tired of earning the virtues of this precept.

This same hasid also served as clerk of the king's treasury, and all the ledgers of the king's secret dealings were entrusted to him. The monarch took his advice in these matters and the hasid was very loyal to his liege in all things.

In the king's court there served a high-ranking minister who was jealous of this Jew, and who strove to ensnare him in some trap which he was to lay for him.

In the hasid's employ was a loyal servant in whom he always placed his trust. One time, however, the minister who hated the hasid bribed this servant with two hundred gold pieces, that he might steal from his innocent hasid master. Thus the manservant took the keys to the chest, there were placed for safekeeping all the king's secret correspondence regarding the treasury, and written matters which the sovereign was not able to transmit to the hasid in person. In this chest were also the confidential letters which the king received from other kings. The minister ordered the servant to steal all the papers and correspondence, every one, and bring it all to him. And so he did, not once and not twice.

Among these papers the minister discovered a document which recorded a certain secret revealed to the hasid by his monarch and of which no other man knew, not even the king's wife. He had written it with his own hand, and asked the hasid to perform a business transaction.

On the morrow, the minister went to the king to discuss a certain matter. As they spoke of this and that, the minister declared this secret before the king.

Surprised, the king said,

- How did you know of this matter?

The minister replied,

- The hasid Jew revealed it to me.

By this, the king saw that the Jew had betrayed his confidence. He was very angry and decided then and there that his clerk of the treasury must die. It was, however, his desire to bring about the hasid's death in a discreet way.

Calling for the hasid Jew, the king entrusted to him a letter addressed to the general of the thousand-man regiment who was posted to guard an area a distance of eight hours from the royal residence. A great wall and a fortified structure were being built there, and all those whom the king did not wish to murder publicly were sent to that place, to their deaths. But this the hasid did not know.

The king wrote to his general as follows, "I am sending you this letter by the hand of a certain man and I hereby deliver him to you. Immediately, when you read this letter, grab the one who has brought this letter and kill him. If he claims that it is not upon him that the king has decreed death, but another man, and that the letter has been given him in error – do not heed and do not listen to him.'

The king signed this letter and gave it to the hasid, saying,

- A private matter has arisen on the subject of which I have written to my regiment commander stationed eight hours distance from here. I do not trust anyone, save yourself, to transmit this letter, therefore do this service for me.

The hasid Jew, together with his trusted servant, immediately harnessed a wagon and set out to bring the letter to the commanding general of the guard.

Mid-way along their journey, four hours from the town and after the noon hour had come and gone and it was close to evening time, one of the village people recognized the hasid, and came to stop his carriage,

- Welcome to you, for you come by here at an auspicious time. My son is eight days old and he must be circumcised on this very day. I sent for a certain mohel but until this moment he has not arrived. It seems certain that he will not arrive today. It being almost evening, I fear that the prescribed hour for the circumcision will pass. If you agree to honor my house by performing this mitzvah, please accompany me, and the virtues of performing the circumcision mitzvah at the correct hour will not be lost to us.

The hasid, in his fervor to participate in the milah covenant, agreed to accompany the man and circumcise his son. But he well knew that the king's instructions for the letter to arrive at its destination must be obeyed. So he placed the letter in the safekeeping of his manservant. After this, he rented another wagon from that town and dispatched his servant to bring the letter to the regiment commander.

And so it was. The hasid performed the circumcision mitzvah at the village, after which he delayed at the home of

"Hear our Prayer" – Raskin

the infant's parent's until a very late hour, sharing in the celebration and the milah feast.

After midnight when the feast was over, the hasid rose and went on his way. Harnessing the wagon, he followed after his servant to the general commandant of the guard's regiment. He had instructed that he await him there after delivering the letter.

He arrived to the commander general's mansion at sunrise. From a distance the general recognized that a carraige of his king's ministers was approaching. Descending from his lookout to welcome the visitor, who did he find but the hasid Jew who was well known to all as one much honored by the king? For the entire kingdom knew that the royal affairs were transmitted into this man's hands.

Before the hasid could speak, the general called out,

- And why did his excellency trouble himself to come here? Did you imagine that I would neglect the king's command? The moment that your servant gave that letter to me, I had him bound and taken to be killed, exactly as was ordered in the king's epistle. I paid no mind to all his explanations and pleas to save himself, and thus fulfilled the command of the king, as written by his own hand.

Only then did the hasid learn that, without his knowledge, he had been rescued from a great evil that had been suspended over his head. The general continued,

- Sir, you did well to came here. I have some news which your servant revealed to me. As I made ready to put him to death, he confessed his sins; he justified and accepted his punishment of death because he had been a traitor and sinned against you. He told me that he stole the keys to your chest and took the king's letters from there, not once and not twice, but many times over. All this was in exchange for the two hundred gold pieces which Minister so-and-so paid him; and your manservant gave all the king's confidential letters to him.

111

When he heard this, the severe expression of the honest hasid was lightened, and he promised the general that he would see to it that the king would raise him in rank.

The hasid returned to his city and came before the king. When the king saw him, he was very surprised and alarmed.

- Where did you come from? And did you not transmit the letter as I instructed?

Thereupon, the hasid related,

- The story unfolds as follows. The Blessed Master of the Universe has excelled in his kindness and compassion. For I learned from the commander general, who heard the confession of my servant, the cause of your anger against me. I know now who laid this snare for me and caused you, to plan my death for no cause. Therefore, your majesty must hurry and send messengers to the home of this certain high-ranking minister. Surprise him and you will remove your letters from his possession before he can learn of what I told you now.

The king immediately dispatched the hasid, accompanied by other royal ministers and judges, to the house of this minister who was caught in the act of perusing the king's confidential correspondence stolen from the hasid. Taken prisoner and brought to the palace, together with his stolen cache, it was decreed by the king that he be put to death. And he was hanged in front of his own house.

More beloved than before by the king, the fortunes of the hasid were increased tenfold. And in him was realized the verse from the Book of Proverbs, of King Solomon, the wisest of men, "The righteous are delivered out of trouble; the wicked come in their stead." And also were realized the words from the Book of Psalms, written by our beloved Psalmist King David, who was the father of Solomon – both beloved of blessed memory – "The hunter's snare has been broken and we are escaped."

The Mitzvah
of Marrying off
a Poor Bride

There was a prominent hasid, highly learned in Torah, who frequented the court of the Maggid Rabbi Yisrael of Kojznitz. It was his habit to travel once a month to be with the Maggid, of blessed memory. This hasid had no children and several times he had asked the rebbe to pray that he might have sons, but the Maggid never said a word.

Now, the hasid's wife troubled him each time he traveled to the rebbe, that he entreat the holy man to help them, and the hasid put her off. One time her tears were so profuse, and she pleaded that on his next visit her husband not depart from Kojznitz until the rebbe responded to his appeal. And she wept that that her life was not worth living if she was to remain without issue for eternity. Perhaps the rebbe would tell her husband that they must divorce, since she could not birth him a child.

So, the hasid was forced to promise his mate that he would obey the decision of the rebbe, no matter what. He

113

traveled to the Maggid Rabbi Yisrael and told him that he was weary of bearing his wife's tears and shouts,

- I stay here in Kojznitz, until the rebbe tells me the solution to my problem. At that, Rabbi Yisrael let a word pass his lips,

- If you agree to forego all your wealth, you will be blessed with sons. But you will always remain a pauper.

Then hasid said,

- I will go and take advice with my wife.

He returned home and related to his wife what Rabbi Yisrael had said. Now the choice was hers to make. She said to her husband,

- What will be will be. I wish to bequeath a remnant for the next generations after I pass from this world! As for the cost, I care not; for the Almighty One who gives life will grant us our livelihood.

The man returned to the Rebbe with the reply that his wife agreed to the conditions, if only she be granted the seed of eternal life. At this Rabbi Yisrael said,

- So be it. Prepare yourself to travel. A long journey awaits you. Take all your ma'ot, for the journey will be costly, and I will tell you what to do. You must travel to the city of Lublin and tell Rabbi Reb' Yaakov Yitzchak that I have sent you to him. He will instruct you further. Now, no matter to what pursuit he directs you, obey all that he says.

Again the man returned home. There he tied together a great knot of money which he secreted on his person, after which he journeyed to Lublin, and arrived at the house of Rabbi Yaakov Yitzchak Ha-Hozeh of Lublin, of blessed memory.

- The Maggid of Kojznitz has sent me to you, that you might instruct me. What am I to do so that my wife shall birth my sons and daughters?

- Sit here until I instruct you.

The hasid remained at a hostelry room in that city for

many days, and thereby used up much of his knot of money. After a while, Rabbi Reb' Yaakov Yitzchak, the Seer of Lublin – so called because he had great power to reveal the genealogy of person's soul and discern its tikkun at each stage of existance – said to the unhappy man,

- The Maggid of Kojznitz perceived skillfully and saw the problem. I have observed you and now understand his intention. Therefore, I will explain the substance of your true problem. . . In your early youth, you were betrothed to certain girl who was to be your bride. When you matured, she appeared tiresome to you and so you severed the betrothal link. By this reason, you have no sons. And, until the time that you ask forgiveness of your betrothed you will have no children. Now, since the woman who was meant for you has wandered far from the place where you both were youths, you must travel a long distance and search her out, until you find her. To make your journey more light, and because I take pity on you, I offer you some fine advice. In about two months time, there will be a market fair in the city of Balta in Bessarabia, and there you will surely find the woman you seek. Go there, and during all the days of market fair search until you find her.

The hasid was relieved and glad that the Rabbi had revealed this to him. Thereupon, he traveled at his ease to the city of Balta, and pondered during his journey, "Perhaps I may meet her along the way. Then I can return to my home even before the market days of Balta." But all his questioning about his former fiancé were to no avail. He arrived in the city of Balta and hired a room. He made no effort to conduct business, since he trusted the Maggid Yisrael of Kojznitz that he would never be a wealthy man again. Also, he was a stranger to the city and had no idea what merchandise to deal in there. Most of the day he remained in his room and prayed for a good outcome. Three hours a day every day, he wandered about the streets of the city. Perhaps he might hear some word of this woman for whom he searched. This was his practice for two months' time, and then the market fair opened. On the first fair day, the hasid walked the streets from morning to night, seeking and asking and still he heard nothing. If not for the rabbi's promise that he would find his former fiancé, his extreme sorrow would have caused him deep discouragement. But he was firm in his decision that he had not come to Balta for naught. So he continued to do what he must do, and was constant in his search. Daily, he asked every new person who came to town if they had knowledge of the woman, but none gave response to his search.

On one of the last three days of the market fair, when all began to depart for home, he found himself standing in one street, confused as what to do. The fair was soon over, and there was no one to help him. A heavy rain began to fall and he ran towards one of the shops to seek shelter. Unable to enter the shop, he stood at the side with others seeking shelter from the rain. And there was one woman, dressed in silk and embroidery and bedecked in many jewels, standing near to him. Out of modesty, he stepped backwards to place distance between them, and she said to her friend,

- Look. This is a man whom I knew in my youth and who distanced himself from me then. Now again he runs from me.

When he heard this, he drew close and asked her, - What did you say?

And she replied,

- It is so. I am as forgotten to you as a dead person is forgotten by the years. Do you not remember the daughter of so-and-so with whom you were bound in a nuptial agreement for four years long? For I am that very woman, who stands next to you here. I was your bethrothed. Now tell me what you are doing here; what has happened with your life; and do you have children?

The hasid opened his heart to her,

- I will not conceal the truth. It is for your sake that I have come to this place. For I have no children, and the saintly Rabbi of Lublin told me that I would have no sons and daughters until I ask your forgiveness. Hear me out, I am prepared to perform any penalty which you will command me. Please forgive the wickedness I did you, and I will bless you that you may never again know sadness such as I caused to you. The woman replied, - The Lord has blessed me and I have all the things I wished for; I have no need of the marriage dowry price or of any gift from you. But, I do have an unfortunate brother, a man of Torah learning, who lives in a certain village, near to the city of Sovalk. He was to marry off his daughter, but now has remained without even one kopek for this purpose. If you wish me to pardon you with all my heart, you must go there and give him 200 gold coins. Then you will surely be blessed and have children.

But the hasid pleaded with her,

- Take what you will from me now and send it on to your brother. Do not burden me with this additional journey. Believe me, I have lost all my fortune traveling here and there in search for you. Will you burden me with this additional journey of several parasangs?. Is it not enough that you take this money from my hand and send it to your brother by mail? She replied,

- I cannot mail this money to my brother since he declared himself a public debtor and those to whom he owes will grab hold of the money at the very moment they hear word of it. Then still he will not be able to marry off his daughter, while I personally am unable to travel at this time. No, No. It is you who must go there. Make your own decision, but keep in mind my terms: you must deliver the money directly into his hand. The moment the money comes into his possession, I will pardon you with all my heart. In addition, this mitzvah of providing him with the money to bring his daughter under the bridal canopy will add more vigor to your actions and good deed. Thereby doubly ensuring that you are granted sons who will be Torah scholars.

The woman concluded,

- I have no more time to stand here and wait for the rain to cease. I go now and we will not meet again. I travel immediately from this place. Should you look for me, you will never again find me. Therefore, do what I have advised: go directly to my brother and, with the help of the Almighty, you will be rescued from your troubles.

She parted from the hasid with a blessing,

- Salutations to my brother from his sister, and wish him well. Now, be on your way and go in peace.

She turned to go and when he tried to follow her, she looked back for a moment, and he heard her say,

- For naught do you follow, and you will never find me again.

She disappeared from his view in mid-street and he saw her no more.

The hasid returned to his hostel to arrange for the wagon journey to Vilna, thinking to himself, "The matter has not been for naught after all. All that happened today is a wonder! " This strengthened his resolve and his devout faith. Hiring a wagon to Vilna and from there to the city of Sovalk, he finally arrived at the village where the brother of his former fiancé lived. He went to his house and there found the brother very troubled. The man was pacing up and down his rooms, caught up in the turmoil of his thoughts. So much so, that he did not observe or greet his guest with the customary salutation in Israel of "Shalom, peace be to you." The hasid spoke,

- Are you Reb' Leib of the city of Sovalk?
- Yes, I am.
- And why are you so beset with despair, which I can see with my own eyes?

118

Wedding Ceremony – M. Oppenheim

- What do you want of me and why do you ask?

The hasid persisted,

- What are your affairs and your worries? Tell me!

But the brother was reluctant to lay bare his heart to this stranger. The hasid implored anxiously that the brother reveal the sorrow of his soul. And he promised that he was able to be the man's rescue, with the help of the Almighty who is the Source of all Blessing.

After much entreaty, the brother spoke,

- Here it is! I have matched my daughter in marriage with one wealthy Jew from Sovalk, and I promised three hundred rubles as my daughter's dowry, in addition to the usual gifts and clothing. I had this sum at the ready, but this year the village proprietor demanded a great deal more money than previously for his rent. He particularly insisted that I pay all his money one year in advance. I was obliged to do so, because the livelihood of mh family is dependent on him. So, I gave the village proprietor all the money which he demanded.

- Now, the time set for the wedding has come and gone. My daughter is, praise G-d, ready for marriage. Yesterday I received the nuptial contract from the father of the groom, together with a letter stating that if I do not pay him the entire dowry within three days' time, he will sever the marriage bonds and arrange a marriage for his son with another bride.

- Now my daughter weeps and sighs and refuses solace, while I pace up and down in my room, my soul desolate, for I am assailed and there is nothing which I can do. I have not one possession to pawn in exchange for the price of this vast dowry. And, believe me that the groom is an extremely fine young man. There is none like to him in all the town. Woe to me, I am truly distraught, and I am also without friends or relatives in this place, for I was born in a far-away city. From where will my help come?

- This is the tale of my extreme wretchedness and aching heart.

The hasid listened carefully and knew now the truth of his former fiance's words to him. Then he said,

- I will give you two hundred gold coins which will be sufficient for all the marriage needs, and there will be money left over.

The brother was amazed,

- But why does a man whom does not know me find such favor in your eyes? Or perhaps you mock me? For never have I seen or heard that even one of the great patricians of this city gave over such a great sum to one man.

The time had come for the hasid to explain,

- I will tell you the truth. I have been sent to you by your sister, Esther Shapira, who instructed me to give you the two hundred gold coins.

- Where did you see my sister? And when did she tell you this thing?

- About three weeks ago I met her at the market fair in the city of Balta. She told me that the time has come when you must marry off your daughter and you have not the means to do so. Your sister was once my intended, and I abandoned the match. At this time, I searched her out in order to ask her forgiveness. But she refused to absolve me until I traveled here to give you two hundred gold coins. I asked that she send it by mail, but she refused, insisting that I myself must go. This is why I traveled to you directly from Balta.

The brother of Esther Shapira, hearing the words of his guest, grew very angry, saying,

- You mock me! You have come here to increase my misery, to remind me of my sister who is dead these 15 years. And was it not myself who buried her? Now you tell me this fiction in her name, a thing which never was.

When the hasid heard these words, he was astonished,

- I swear that I have not come to ridicule you! I speak only the truth. Or perhaps there is a mistake, and you are not the brother of the woman Esther Shapira whom I was to marry. Please tell me. Are you Reb Leib of Sovalk, the son of Eliezer?

Then he indicated all the signs given to him by the sister. Wonderingly the brother replied,

- I am that man whom you seek. But what imagined tale has come to your mind, or was it in a dream that you envisioned my sister in Balta. For, one thing is certain – my sister is dead. If you do not believe me, I will take you to her grave.

More and more astounded, the hasid truly understood now what was the purpose of all his effort, as brought about by the Maggid Rabbi Yisrael of Kojznitz,

- I can see that the Almighty has sent me on this errand and directed this money to you who have earned it in order to perform the mitzvah of marrying your daughter. Yes, you are the man whom I seek.

Then he told him his entire tale from beginning to end. That the Maggid of Kojznitz had sent him to Lublin, to Rabbi Reb' Yaakov Yosef who directed him to the city of Balta. There he searched for Esther Shapira her but did not find her, until she herself found him.

A great trembling took hold of the brother,

- Draw her likeness and her costume. If the figure is familiar to me, I will know it was indeed my own sister.

The hasid did this, thus-and-thus was she, and the brother recognized his sister.

- This is truly my sister Esther, and I can see that the Almighty has dispatched her to help me in my time of trouble. Now, by virture of your help in performing the mitzvah of paying the bridal costs, the Lord will surely shower his blessings upon you. May you bring forth sons who are great scholars, and learned in Torah. Thus will you be granted new life, just as you have granted me life. As it is

122

said, "One who saves a life in Israel, it is as though he has saved an entire world."

The hasid submitted to the brother the gold coins that were meant for him, and they parted in peace. When he returned to his home, he related to the Maggid Rabbi Yisrael of Kojznitz all the chronicles of this tale.

A Russian Jew – H. Struck

One Mitzvah Paves the Way for the Next

D uring the lifetime of the Kadosh Rabbi Baruch of Medzibezh, of blessed memory, who was the grandson of the Ba'al Shem Tov, a great trouble and a terrible sickness fell upon Israel – may the Almighty save us from catastrophe. The Israelites appealed to the rebbe that he might pray to the Almighty for this death to be removed from them. And, the rebbe instructed them thus,

- Travel several parasangs distance to the neighboring village, and there search out one man whose name is as follows, and whose father was such-and-such. Do not depart that place until this man declares that the Lord has removed this trouble.

The men departed their homes and city, considering in their hearts,

- Without doubt, this person must be a great and marvelous zaddik, since our righteous rebbe has sent us to him that he might issue a good edict. For it is well known that the Almighty carries out the bidding of the zaddik.

They did as their rebbe had bidden them. When they had traveled a distance and arrived to a certain town, all asked the townspeople where the home of this zaddik whose name is as follows and his father's name was such-and-such. But, the villagers' reply was,

- In our village, no wonder-zaddik with such a name can be found.

At this the travelers were very surprised, because their faith in their meritorious rebbe was strong and they knew that he did not speak hollow words. Therefore, they were firmly decided to search for this man. Seeking out and inquiring, finally one Jew approached them,

- And what do you need with such a drunkard as this? For he lies prostrate on his pallet and knows not the difference between his right and his left.

These Jews on a mission to cure the evil plague went to the house of that man. There they told his wife that their sainted rebbe had sent them. The man's wife said,

- I laugh to see whom you seek. For he is lying here and sleeping off his drunken stupor.

Out of the bitterness of her spirit, she related her husband's tale. Once a very wealthy man, there came a day when he began to devote himself to the bitter drop, and soon he fell into poor times. Since then, it was habit to down whiskey from the minute he rose from slumber. Then he would drink again, until he fell onto the pallet in an excess of drunkenness. And this had been his way for many years.

- If you wish to talk with him, wait until he rises from sleep. Soon he will seek out another glass of grog, and having done, will fall asleep straight away.

The emissaries from Rabbi Baruch of Medzibezh were very surprised to hear these things. Asking question after question regarding this man's customs and manner, they did not find him to contain even the most paltry jot of good and holiness. And, it was only by reason of their great faith in

126

their rebbe that they waited there until they had almost lost hope.

As soon as this drunkard awoke, he reached out for a glass of whiskey. The visitors hurried over to him, saying that the zaddik rebbe of Medzibezh had sent them to him, that he might remove the power of an evil sickness from Israel. The drunkard said,

- First I will have a drop of whiskey.

- You will not move from here and we will not permit you to drink whiskey until you decree what we have asked.

Thereupon, he lifted his head and stated clearly,

- The Makom who is Everywhere, in His great compassion will remove the sickness from our brethren, the house of Israel.

So they let him be and went on their way, returning to their city of Medzibezh. Every one of them observed and noted well the hour of the day they returned. Because it was as the drunkard had declared – in one instant, the plague lifted, and the matter was wondrous in their eyes.

When they came into the presence of their esteemed rebbe, they asked that he reveal to them the secret and enigma of it. For he had sent them to a man who was an extreme drunkard, a man abased in the eyes of all who knew him. Even his wife viewed him with disfavor, as did all the Jews of that town. In other words, this was a man who was not concentrated on his own behavior. Therefore, what was the meaning of it?

Their rebbe explained,

- Stay a while and I will relate the power of one mitzvah which this man performed. He once was a wealthy and successful merchant, of handsome bearing and a pleasing countenance. One day, he visited the widow of a certain important state official on business, and when she saw him, she longed in her heart that his fine looks become her own. So she said to him,

- "You will be my husband and I will be your wife. For what good is the wife who is with you now? I offer you my money and gold, the valuable fortune of my home and all my shares in this land – field and vineyard – will be yours. In addition, if you accept my proposal, you can serve as a high government minister, and become heir to the position of my late husband. You will surely advance higher in position than the other ministers, because you are very intelligent."

- The man accepted her proposal,

- "I am prepared to consent, but I impose one condition. Firstly, that you prepare a great feast, and invite the ministers and other notables; that they might witness and recognize me from that day forward as an important official and a minister of the land."

- She agreed, and the Jew went to prepare himself for the specified day. He would arrive for the feast and then marry her, because he too wished her to be his wife and longed to enjoy much honor.

- The day arrived. A magnificent feast was made ready and many ministers invited, with the future minister hosted at their head. At daybreak, when the feast was over and all the guests gone home, the Jewish merchant had not yet taken the lady as his wife. He wished to have a stroll to refresh himself and enjoy the courtyard of that grand mansion. While walking, he heard loud wailing and groaning resounding from a dank enclosure of the courtyard. These were the voices of Israelites imprisoned for not having paid taxes to the lady of the mansion on the assigned date. They cried in aloud,

- "Hoi, hoi, have pity on us!"

- But no one heard them, and no one responded. His compassion was aroused, and he hurried to the guards, demanding that the people groaning in this house be freed. And so it was. Harnessing horses to a carriage, he returned them to their homes as free men and in peace.

128

- When he had performed this important mitzvah of freeing prisoners, it worked the way of all mitzvot – that one mitvah leads the way to a second, and so on. In other words, he began to think to himself, "What am I doing here, to abandon my wife and become a husband of a foreign woman? I have sinned before the Almighty, G-d forbid, that I might perform such a wicked act.'

- He hurried to hire the best horses and wagon, and escaped from that place before he might be tempted to carry out this sin.

- Now because this man had performed the mitzvah of ransoming prisoners, and also had repented in that place and overcome temptation from the woman, the heavenly court ruled that this man was from that time on considered and declared a zaddik, who would have the power to govern the high matters of the material world. For what the zaddik decrees the Almighty will enact. In other words, the heavenly court would be required to carry out the edicts of this man's lips.

- Then began a great uproar in the celestial household. If this would be so, all decrees would be cancelled and the rule of justice removed in its entirety.

- It was decided to make an exception in the case of this man. The celestial prosecutor was given leave to have his say during the man's lifetime. Thus, he was judged in the full strictness of law, and the verdict taken that he must from that time on live his life as a drunkard, forever retarded by his drink; during his lifetime he would not know rest or peace and would be unaware of the goings on in the world.

Truth to tell, it was a great danger to approach him, since he had the authority to summon decrees which the ministering angels were obliged to obey. However, because of the severity of this plague, and so that the terrible sickness might cease, the drunkard-of-the-mitzvah was permitted by the decision of Rabbi Baruch of Medzibezh to let loose his vast power. Then the zaddik commanded and the Almighty harkened and obeyed.

Let all Suspicion be Unfounded

I n this manner does it appear in the ancient ledger of the Jewish community of Chortkov, as regards Reb' Meyer Amschel, the wealthy and renowned first patrician of the house of Rothschild. When Reb' Meyer Amschel was a bachur, he ministered in the sacred service of Rabbi Zvi-Hirsch HaLevi Ish Horowitz, the Presiding Judge of the Jewish court of Chortkov. Dayyan Ish Horowitz had a daughter whose time it would be soon to enter the bridal canopy, and for this purpose he had set aside a cache of five hundred gold coins. He kept his daughter's dowry, hidden in a compartment of his writing table which he rarely had cause to open.

Once a year, on the 14th day of the Hebrew month of Nissan, prior to the Passover festival, the house was carefully scrutinized for any remaining crumb of leavened bread or other hametz foods, which are strictly forbidden to the Jews during all the days of Passover. Then, the Rav would open this compartment and be reassured that the money cache was safe.

One year, his shammash, Reb' Meyer Amschel of the Jewish community of Snyatyn, took a wife. He purchased a shop and soon his small business began to show a profit. Soon thereafter, he decided to leave the service of Rabbi Zvi-Hirsch.

The eve of the 14th of Nissan which followed the departure of his shammash from service, when the rabbi came to examine his money cache in the compartment of his writing table, the pouch containing the 500 gold coins was gone. He and the members of his household were startled by this and became greatly agitated. His family decided that the thief could be no one else but Reb' Meyer Amschel, the proof being that he had purchased a shop and word had it that he was doing increasingly well. Surely, it was the ma'ot he had stolen which made this success possible.

Rabbi Zvi Hirsch silenced them repeatedly,

- You suspect an innocent and a kosher man, for I know my attendant well. All the time that he served in this house, his ways were the ways of an honest and a G-d fearing man. He was faithful to our family and to our home. Forbid that a man should be suspected of a crime to which he has no connection.

However, the members of the Rabbi's household gave him no peace, insisting that it could be only this particular person who had stolen the pouch and secreted the money among his belongings. They continued to persuade and influence him, and finally he was urged to seek out and speak to Reb' Amschel; to clarify the matter and see if it was so.

It was against his will that Rabbi Zvi-Hirsch journeyed to Snyatyn. And when the man who had served in faithful attendance to his Rabbi, and loved him without limits or boundaries saw him there, he rejoiced and made much effort to honor him exceedingly. After a while, Rabbi Zvi-Hirsch raised the subject of his money cache. Layers were

132

The Rothschild Family at Prayer - Moritz Daniel Oppenheim

uncovered and covered again, until finally the shape of his suspicion took form.

When Reb' Meyer Amschel understood the subject of this visit, he immediately said,

- Yes, the money has been taken from you, and I was the one who did this thing. Although presently I do not have more than 200 gold coins in hand, I give these to you, sir, here and now. Within a set interval I will repay all that I have taken from you.

The Rabbi returned home happily. Not only was his family not to blame for casting aspersion on the guiltless, but also the loss would be returned to its master. His shammash would dispatch to him a sum of gold coins at each alloted interval.

Now, the custom in Israel is to embark on household repairs and to whitewash all the rooms during the weeks before Passover. As it was in the household of Rabbi Zvi-Hirsch HaLevi Ish Horowitz.

In the year that the gold coins disappeared, a local farm woman from a neighboring village of Chortkov had been hired to help with the pre-Passover chores. When the rabbi had opened the compartment in his table, as was his custom at that time of year, this woman was in the room and observed the pouch of money hidden there. Setting her eye upon it, she later stole into the compartment, opening it with a key and taking the pouch with all the ma'ot, which she brought to her husband. The husband secreted the pouch away, and for a long while the incident was hidden from everyone's knowledge.

Much time passed, and when the farmer considered that the incident was forgotten, he was tempted to finally to enjoy his theft. At first, he removed only one coin from the purse. This he brought with him to the tavern in the town, to purchase whiskey to comfort his heart and the hearts of his comrades. Time came to pay the tavern keeper, and he handed him the gold coin,

- Here you are. I found this coin. Go to town and change it for me, take what is coming to you for the drink and return the change to me.

And so it was. The following week, the farmer went to the tavern to again drink his fill. He brought out another gold coin from inside his shift,\ saying to the tavern-keeper that he had found it as well. On the third week, it was more of the same. The tavern-keeper, observing this farmer two times and three to remove gold coins from his shift, well understood that these were not as pebbles cast in the road for all to find. He began to consider, "This man is no more than a thief and has stolen all the coins." Immediately, he took himself off to a certain magistrate and related all he had observed.

The magistrate instructed him thus,

- When this farmer next comes to your tavern, douse him well with liquor until he is overtaken with drink. We all know that where wine enters a man's secrets emerge. Surrounded by his drinking mates, he will pour out his tale. And so it was.

When the farmer was muddled with drink and his heart became jolly, his mates asked from where had all these coins come. Much the worse for his liquor, he shared with them the hidden secret of his heart. He revealed that his wife had stolen a pouch of money from the rabbi and that he had buried the remainder of the coins at a certain spot near his house.

The tavern owner heard all this and brought the witnesses, who had also heard the drunkard's tale, with him to the magistrate who immediately dispatched his men to the house of the farmer in the village. Digging in the appointed spot, they uncovered the money pouch from which only several coins were missing. The man was arrested and brought before the magistrate where he admitted his guilt.

Then the magistrate called for Rabbi Zvi-Hirsch, who was very frightened at the summons, and thought, "Who knows what false accusation has been set against myself and my people?"

The magistrate began by questioning him,

- How many sons and daughters do you have? How much is your weekly income?

Rabbi Zvi-Hirsch told him everything he wished to know. Then the magistrate asked,

- And how will you marry off your daughter who is now of age?

The rabbi told him that he had set aside 500 gold coins which he saved for his daughter's dowry and the other wedding needs in a pouch, and this had been stolen from him. The magistrate asked the rabbi to describe the pouch which he did, giving the correct signs. Recognizing that true justice was at work, the magisterate handed the pouch with the gold coins to Rabbi Zvi-Hirsch. Then he explained how the pouch had been stolen from the rabbi's table drawer and how it was found.

Joyously, Ish Horowitz returned home and soon after that set out to the city of Snyatyn to ask his former shammash the why of his behavior in this matter. Why did Reb' Meyer Amschel admit to taking this money when he had never in his life stolen?

In Snyatyn, Reb Meir Anschel explained the truth of his actions. For when he had seen his rabbi deeply unhappy, he knew that to return home without a solution would leave the rabbi and his family sore at heart. For this reason, he decided to accept the burden of guilt for the theft upon his shoulders.

- So I took all the money that I own and sold every possession, sending it straight-away to the rabbi in order to ease the trouble of this zaddik. I had almost to pawn the

136

cushions and chairs of my home in order to continue the payments as I promised.

Dayyan Ish Horowitz asked forgiveness again and again for believing his former shammash a thief. Then he returned all the money paid to him and blessed him, saying,

- For this act of kindness you will prosper and achieve great wealth. The fortune you assemble shall serve your family for many generations to come.

From that day forward, Reb' Meyer Amschel began to prosper exceedingly in all his ventures and endeavors. His family became very famous, and are today the well known and affluent House of Rothschild.

Visiting the Sick

All Things are Perceived

One woman came to the Rabbi Yehudelle of Greidung in tears, pleading that the excellent zaddik trouble himself to visit her severely ill husband. The man was dying and not able to leave his house, and there was a very important matter which he must discuss with the zaddik before he left this world.

Rabbi Yehudale consented to visit the sick man and together with several of his hasidim, they accompanied the wife home. Arriving at the house of the sick man, the rabbi opened the door to enter and immediately became alarmed. He stepped back and, closing the door, stood silently for several moments outside the threshold. Only then did he open the door again and enter to sit beside the sick man.

The man began to weep bitterly before him, saying that he knew that he was dying and going the way of all earthly man, and alas, he had no meritorious acts in his soul to protect and recommend him when he arrived in the world to come.

The rabbi asked whether he could recall at least one good act which he had performed during his lifetime,

- If so, tell it to me.

The sick man thought and thought, and then said that he had no praiseworthy act to tell of. He was totally unlearned; the one single prayer which he knew, he was able to recite only in the most simple manner. He had made his living as a tanner of hides removed from cattle after they were ritually slaughtered for meat.

Again the rabbi asked that he attempt to remember any meritorious act. And the rabbi asked the same question a third time.

The sick man was silent for several moments, and suddenly he began to tell the rabbi a tale,

- Here! I do recall a good deed, a small thing which I once did. One day, I rose to go to my labors, and along my route I saw a wagon dash down the mountain loaded down with men, women and children returning from a wedding in the town. The wagon master was drunk and was unable to rein in the horses who had strayed from the straight road to the sides of the incline. The wagon and its load raced wildly down the mountainside and on each side of the road was a steep slope which dropped into a deep ravine. Because of the heavy weight of the wagon and all the people it in it, the horses could not cease the plunge down into the chasm. One could see that all would crash at the bottom of the cliff and their bones be broken, G-d forbid.

- Seeing this, that these people were about to be crushed in life and limb, I ran quickly over to the wagon. Taking my life in my hands, with all my strength I grabbed hold of the horses' reins and balanced the wagon on my back. Thus, I delayed its plunge forward just long enough for the people to jump out. I immediately let the wagon and the horses go free, and the wagon with all its contents twisted off the road. The horses were killed and the wagon was broken into small pieces. But all the passengers were saved by me.

- This is a small thing which I remember that. Except for

140

this, there is no superior act that I can recall which could serve to recommend me when I come to the world of truth.

The rabbi comforted the dying man and also instructed him to visit him in a dream after death. He wished to learn what had been decided in the celestial court. The sick man promised to fulfill his request.

When Rabbi Yehudelle returned to his home, the hasidim accompanying him asked why he had become alarmed and had recoiled from the door after opening it, then closed the door and waited some time before he opened again to enter.

The Rabbi replied,

- I had been certain that I was going to visit one of the simple people. But, when I opened the door, I saw before me a candelabra of fire suspended over the sick man's head. Seven flames burned there, and this is customary only regarding a great zaddik. Naturally, I was shocked and had to retreat. I closed the door to calm myself a bit. When I was prepared, I opened the door to enter. That is the reason why I asked the dying man to relate of his meritorius acts, once, twice and three times. I understood that he was a zaddik nistar, a mystical and hidden saintly man.

- After my third question, he recalled the tale of saving all the people in that wagon. Know that he did this with great sacrifice, since he himself could easily have been killed when he ran to halt this heavy load from crashing down the mountain slope with only his shoulder. And the Almighty came to his assistance, for the man was saved from death, and all the passengers with him. By the power of an unselfish act performed with supreme devotion by this simple man – he earned a wonderous reward. That is the vision of the burning candalabra which I saw suspended over his head.

After this simple man of the people died, he appeared to Rabbi Yehudelle in a dream one night and told him,

- The celestial court did not allow me to enter the Garden of Eden until I fulfilled the promise which I made to you.

141

And that was to relate what happened when I came before the celestial court. And so, after I died, the court weighed my earnings and debits on the two sides of the scale. The virtues were not many and the weight of my debts, which were too numerous to count, burdened the scale against me.

- As my earnings and my debts were being weighed, a wagon arrived, loaded down with men, women and children and this wagon was placed onto the side of my earnings. The great weight of this wagon and its load of people, together with the mud clinging to the wheel spokes, changed the balance to the side of my earnings which now greatly outweighed my debits. Therefore, the heavenly court declared that I was to go to Gan Eden. But when I arrived at the entrance to Gan Eden, I was not given entry until I fulfilled my promise which I made to speak to you in a dream.

- Now, I ask you, the Zaddik Rabbi so exalted in Torah, to forgive me, for I have not been given permission to disclose more than what I have already said or to tell anything at all of that world. The right has not been given me to reveal that which has been forbidden to reveal.

Let my Soul be Humble as the Dust

Rabbi Hanoch Hanich Ha-Kohen of Alexander, an outstanding student of Rabbi Simhah Bunem of Przysucha, once told his hasidim, - If you wish to know to what level of modesty a man can aspire, observe a circumstance which befell Rabbi Abraham Abish, the Presiding Judge and Chief Rabbi of the Beit Din of Frankfurt on the Main.

It was the habit of Rabbi Abraham Abish to occupy himself with the mitzvah of charity and all manner of assistance to the poor. For this aim, he was accustomed to come and go at the homes of wealthy Jewish notables and to seek out merchants from the outlying areas who visited his city on business matters during the important fairs. In this way, he took himself from place to place throughout the city, knocking on the doors of any likely philanthropist and collecting alms for the poor and the widows and orphans whom the Torah most strictly specifies that the community is obligated to protect.

It happened one time that Rabbi Abish entered one of the

lodginghouse chambers where a traveling Jewish merchant was resting. This merchant sat at the table perusing his account ledgers and was very occupied with his thoughts. When Rabbi Abraham Abish approached him to appeal for a generous contribution for the poor of his city, that man did not listen or turn his face in the rabbi's direction. This merchant did not know that the man standing before him was the Rav D'mata, the Chief Rabbi of the Jewish community of Frankfurt on the Main. This was a very large city populated with wise and learned men, teachers of Torah and writers of holy books, who were well known throughout all the lands of Jewish dispersion. The good name of this rabbi had spread far and wide.

His preoccupation with account books caused him not attend his heart even for one moment to address the man standing before him. The rabbi, on his part, did not announce his own name or title, as it was not his nature to consider himself a personage. Rabbi Avraham Abish did not believe that he had an advantage over his fellow man by reason of occupying the chair of Chief Rabbi of Frankfurt. And this is how it came about that the merchant erred grievously. He rudely dispatched the Chief Rabbi from his presence and turned him away, certain that this was a mere pauper who begged alms from door to door to keep his soul alive.

- Do not trouble me. Go on your way.

By reason of the rabbi's excellent qualities of humility and saintliness, he did not press the merchant. He turned from the man, his countenance revealing no emotion, and left that place.

Soon the merchant rose from his chair and, preparing to go out into the street, he looked for his walking stick where he had placed it in the corner of the room just a short while ago, but did not find it there. Now this walking stick was very precious to him and he loved it dearly. Certain that the

Listening to the Rebbe - Henia Steinberg

"pauper" who had just left his presence had stolen it as an act of revenge for not having been given alms, the merchant was filled with rage. Immediately he made up his mind to chase after this pauper and have the stolen walking stick returned to him.

Running out into the street as quickly as he could, he followed Rabbi Abish and caught up with him not far from the lodginghouse, whereupon he began to shout and pour his wrath upon him,

- What a thief! Give me the stick which you stole because I refused to give you alms!

The Rabbi replied in his humble manner,

- G-d forbid that I should have done such a thing . . . to steal something from you? Trust me, I know nothing of this thing.

This he repeated several times and then asked that the merchant leave him in peace

But the merchant's increased ire burning within him at this act of thievery, really caused him to believe that the man standing before him had stolen his walking stick and gone off to secret it in some safe hiding place. He lifted his arm, and brought it down vigorously upon the head and shoulders of the Chief Rabbi of Frankfurt on the Main. The Rav D'mata accepted the beating with the love and modest humility which was his nature, and did not respond or retaliate to the sounds of his own humiliation.

Several days went by, and this merchant was delayed in Frankfurt on matters of business and commerce. One day he learned that on the holy Sabbath the Chief Rabbi Avraham Abish, was to expound on subjects of Aggadah and Halachah at the central bet midrash, as was his habit on certain occasions. All the Jewish community was to gather there to hear the learned sermon. The merchants of the town and the outlying areas would be sure to come to enjoy the pleasing words of that zaddik who was well-known throughout the land.

This merchant who, unknown to himself, had already taught the Chief Rabbi the force of his arm, was taken with a longing and an aspiration to hear the sermon. On Shabbos, he readied himself to enter the study hall. The rabbi had begun to address the congregation. When the merchant crossed the threshold and looked to the podium to observe the great man's face, he saw and recognized that the rabbi was that very man he had imagined to be a pauper and a poor wretch whom he had accused of stealing his walking stick. He had rudely turned away and dismissed the Chief Rabbi of Frankfurt and then vilified and beaten him.

When he realized his error and the ugly act which had sprung from his hand, he was stricken dumb, and he swooned by reason of sorrow and remorse of heart. For it was as spoken by King Solomon, the wisest of men, "That which is crooked cannot be made straight . . " And he lay on the ground until the members of the congregation standing nearby bent over to arouse him from his faint.

When he returned to consciousness and was asked the cause of his faint, he related all that had transpired. The congregants advised that there was no cure for it but to wait until the rabbi had finished his sermon. As the rabbi would descend from the podium, the merchant must approach and beg his forgiveness with many appeasing words. He must ask his pardon for the terrible thing he had done.

The merchant accepted this advice with all his heart and soul. When the rabbi descended from the dais of the bet midrash and went to sit in his place of honor, the congregants who had come to hear him speak drew close to honor him and shake his hand, saying, as was the custom,

- Wonderful, wonderful! Yasher Ko'ach, May your strength ever increase!

Agitated and trembling, the merchant approached to beg

Rabbi Abraham Abish's forgiveness. He joined in the throng welcoming and congratulating the rabbi, but his heart did not dare and his voice was unable to fulfill its task – his lips moved but no sound was heard.

The rabbi saw the merchant approaching and drawing near and imagined that the man had sought him out to strike him again for stealing his walking stick. Rabbi Abish began to calm him, speaking soft words of appeasement,

- Believe me, my brother, I have no knowledge of the theft of your walking stick, please lay no suspicion of transgression upon me. For, the Almighty forbid it, I did not take your cane and am not aware of who took it. I do not deceive you and it is as true as myself now standing in this holy place.

Thus, the Jews of Frankfurt on the Main witnessed the great modesty of their rabbi. In the very hour that he was embraced by the love of his congregation which had risen to give him honor, he was prepared to abase himself and apologize to the merchant yet another time. For Rabbi Abraham Abish never thought for one moment that the merchant had come to appease him and to ask his pardon.

And the merchant learned the bitter lesson of suspecting an innocent man and thereby casting a blot upon his honor.

Drawing – Tully Filmus

THE GATES OF WISDOM, INSIGHT AND KNOWLEDGE

Prefer The
Wise Man

I n the Year of the Creation five-thousand-three hundred-and-fifteen, the gaon and zaddik who had presided over the Bet Din of Cracow passed away, leaving no heir to take his place.

The days of mourning passed, and for its large and active Jewish community, the grand city of Cracow seemed an abyss — bereft now of a spiritual and halachic master. The leaders of the community sat to consult, and the decision was taken to dispatch emmisaries throughout the land, to search for a greatly learned gaon and zaddik to take on the role of rabbi for their eminent city.

At that time, the rare brilliance and learning of Rabbenu Moshe Leib Isserles, the author of the "Mapa" for the "-Shulchan Aruch", who was then 18 years old, began to be renowned among the Jews. Word of his estimable qualities in Torah had spread throughout the lands of dispersion.

When this news reached the community leaders and parnassim of Cracow, they dispatched a messenger to Rabbi Moshe Isserles and invited him to serve as their Teacher in Justice and spiritual leader. After much beseeching and appeal, he accepted and immediately a splendid carriage was harnessed to a pair of fine horses. All the Jewish

notables of Cracow set out on a journey to visit the rabbi and
to offer their respects. Rabbi Isserles promised the notables
of Cracow that he would come to settle in their community.
On the date agreed upon, they were to dispatch a carriage
for him.

Cracow's Jewish notables returned happily to their city
with the glad tidings that the Almighty had fulfilled their
need. A great Master had accepted the post of rabbi of the
distinguished community of Cracow. On the appointed day
he would arrive and be installed in the rabbinical seat.

The townspeople were joyous, thanking the Almighty,
and all said, "For He is Good and His charity is forever"; for
the Blessed One had not abandoned the esteemed Jewish
community of Cracow. They prayed always to be nourished
in future days by great rabbis, zaddikim and hasidim. And
these were the delegates of the Almighty in the temporal
world.

The community leaders then requested an audience with
the Bishop of Cracow in order to ask his permission that
Rabbenu Moshe serve as their rabbi. Such were the manners
in the city of Cracow at that time; it was not fitting to choose
a rabbi to lead the Jewish community without permission
from the bishop. It was also customary that their Chief Rabbi
led the delegation on occasions that the community hosted
the bishop.

All the parnassim were ushered into the presence of the
bishop, where they explained to him the excellence of
Rabbenu Moshe Isserles, extolling his vast Torah learning
and saying that he was more wise than any other rabbi of his
generation. All the rabbis of the dispersion hastened to
dispatch their homiletic and halachic queries to him and
therefore wisdom and Torah extended from Rabbi Isserles to
all the communities of Israel.

The bishop was very glad to hear these tidings and said to
them,

- If what you say is so, I am very happy that our city will have the honor of being the leader of all the other communities of Israel, since many will travel to the rabbi to seek answers to their queries. I also rejoice that a great man, learned in Torah, valued throughout the lands of the Jewish exile will reside in our city. Your lot is a happy one that you earned the right to appoint such a man to lead you.

- As for myself, my fate has much improved when I hear that Rabbi Isserles has great skill in all wisdoms, that 'his hands are sufficient for him', and that I will gain a friend with whom I can discuss and consider. Therefore, I must be informed of the day he will arrive and you welcome him to Cracow. I wish to greet and accompany him as he enters the city. With me will be an entourage of respected city officials and other noblemen, as suits such a very precious personage as you describe and praise here before me.

The parnassim departed from the bishop's presence happy and reassured, praising the Almighty for the great good He does for Israel.

On the day set, a carriage with ten horses was harnessed at the ready and a livery hired to run before the carraige. These were dispatched to bring Rabbi Isserles. When the news came that he was approaching Cracow, they informed the bishop. Immediately he had his horses harnessed to his own splendid carriage, embellished in gold. Important officials and other nobility joined him and they all set out to greet the rabbi.

From this description, you will understand that no one, except perhaps small infants, remained in all the city of Cracow. For all had come to welcome the rabbi with drums and all manner of musical instruments. Finally the entourage arrived at the city in honor and glory, and a fanfare was sounded out which preceded them, announcing,

- Make way for the honorable Rabbenu Moshe Isserles,

Studying in the small hours of the night - Ira Moscowitz

the Presiding Judge of the Rabbinical Court and the Rabbi of the city of Cracow.

However, when the bishop saw the form and the countenance of the rabbi, who was eighteen years old at that time and bore as yet little sign of a beard, and who was also small and dark-complected in his appearance, he scorned him in his heart, thinking,

- The Jews have erred in their great and exaggerated praise of this one who is no more than an infant not yet burdened in years, and he is small in stature as well!

Much vexed that he had extended honor to such a weanling, the Bishop was silent and did not speak a word until they arrived back in the city. After accompanying the rabbi to the house chosen for him by his community, the bishop called for the Jewish notables and said,

- I have gone to great trouble and you have misled me; to extend so much honor to a weanling, one not yet burdered in years! You spoke countless wonders in his praise, while I do not discern even a tenth of such note in him. Truth to tell, I have been humiliated in the eyes of my assembly and before all my ministers and notables. I have taken the trouble to ride out and welcome a young Hebrew stripling, no more than eighteen years of age, and to extend to him all this honor suitable for kings.

- For this reason I am going to do the following. I decree that throughout all the lands under my authority all men of wisdom and philosophy will gather together in Cracow on a certain day. Now, your rabbi will be obliged to face all these wise men in a debate and he must reply to all the questions they ask him in all the categories of wisdom. If the outcome is that he succeeds in proving his worth and replying to all these scholars and wise men, I will give him respect, as is his due.

- And if, forbid, he will fail and not have solutions for their questions, not only will I extend my hand to kill the rabbi, but

I will also kill all the Jewish community. I shall utterly destroy the women, children and babies all, and all your properties will be set aflame. This by reason of your having made a mockery of myself and all my ministers and even my servants. All this I will do. I have spoken and will not leave a trace of the Jews in all the city of Cracow, if you do not make good in this debate.

The parnassim departed from the bishop, their hearts astounded and appalled. Joy had become bitter mourning. Consulting with one another in confidence, all agreed that they must declare a fast day for the Jews, a day on which the people would unite to call out to the Almighty with all their hearts. But, so as to conceal the matter from Rabbi Moshe Isserles – for they wished to prevent sorrow and grief from his soul – all the people were cautioned that Rabbenu Moshe not be told. After the conclusion of the fast they would inform him that it had been decreed that the rabbi must debate against many of the Bishop's wise men and prove his wisdom over their own.

On the day of the fast, Rabbenu Moshe observed that his servants and the members of his household did not partake of food, and the countenance of each was etched with distress. He called upon his servants and ordered them to relate the casue for this. Thus, they revealed the truth and told him all that had transpired with the bishop. When the rabbi heard these matters, and that the joy of all the Jews of his community had turned to mourning, he immediately sent messengers to announce throughout the town that all must eat and drink. No one was to be overly concerned.

Then he came before them and said,

- From the day you accepted me as your rabbi, it is forbidden that you declare a fast without my authority. For this reason, although you took this fast upon yourselves in good faith, it is valueless, since I declare it null and void. This is especially so because my faith in the Almighty, who is the source of all blessing, is boundless. I am certain that He will help me prevail in this debate, and I will respond to every challenge put before me.

Hearing this, the Jews of Cracow rejoiced. They gave glory to the Lord in their hearts and praised their rabbi. The bishop was notified that Rabbi Moshe Isserles had agreed without apprehension to compete with him and his deputies in the debate.

The bishop immediately dispatched runners to all the provinces under his influence, that priests and bishops and other Christian philosophers might come on the appointed date to his city. Choosing the community secretariat as premises for the debate, all the people came to see and to hear, and the bishop also came there. Then he dispatched one of his ministers in a carriage harnessed to two horses to bring the rabbi to the secretariat.

When the rabbi saw the carriage with only one minister in it, he said,

- I do not serve a bishop who sends for me in a carriage suitable only for those of small worth. I am the head of all the communities of the dispersion of Israel. In particular, I am the head of the Cracow Jewish community. My honor is their own. Therefore, I will not agree to ride in your carriage, lest I diminish the honor due to the Torah. Please tell your bishop that if he wishes for me to I participate in this debate, he will take care not to slur my honor, especially since his side has not gained the upper hand yet in the debate. When he sends for me, he should consider well that he sends for the Chief Rabbi of the Jews of Cracow.

The messenger returned to the bishop with the message from Rabbi Isserles. This behavior very much appealed to the bishop and he thought, "It is clear that this rabbi is very clever and he knows well the kind of honor that is due to the one superior in value." The bishop then huried to dispatch a carriage harnessed to six horses with liveried servants running before it, and they were accompanied by ministers and other notables, to honor and welcome him.

Rabbi Moshe Isserles agreed to ride in this carriage. They arrived at the secretariat and the rabbi could see that the building was filled with people from end to end. He entered there, secure in his faith in the Almighty and without the least bit of fear, just as a man enters his own home. He sat himself at the head of the table which had been prepared and the bishop was already seated there, at his side. The bishop said to him,

- I intended, in truth, to seat you here at the head of all these people. However, in my opinion, it is not polite that a man choose the seat of honor at his own will.

Then Rabbenu Moshe replied,

- I well know that you have prepared all this fine glory for me. Indeed, all have come here to hear the words of my mouth. By reason of this fact, it is only the way of the earth that no man insults me by showing me my appointed seat. Rather I sit in the place which I have chosen.

This made the bishop quite angry, but he bided his time until the outcome would be known. Instructing his scholars to begin the debate, they proceeded to question the rabbi in all the seven measures of wisdom. They debated for several days, and to each wise man's questions, the rabbi replied with few and select words. Soon the philosophers and scholars found themselves outwitted. All their powers of reason were not victorious over him.

For his part, the bishop was thrilled by the words of wisdom spoken by Rabbenu Moshe. All the philosophers and wise men were forced to admit the rabbi's superior wisdom. Then the bishop said to him,

- Thanks be to you, for now I have learned that there exists the merit of faith in the Jewish nation. I see that the truth of even half your real wisdom and the heights to which it reaches, was not imparted to me. I, therefore, extend to you the honor which you deserve and declare hereby that all the days of my life you will serve as father and patron to me. And that, as Pharoah of Egypt said to Joseph, "According to your word shall my people be ruled."

And this is how Rabbi Moshe Isserles also gained the honor and respect of the Bishop and all the ministers and citizens of the city of Cracow.

A Difficult Passage of the Talmud – I. Snowman

I The Lord am Your Physician

There was a man of great wealth, one of the Jewish patricians and wealthy notables of the city of Vilna, who was journeying through the city of Mezhirech during the routine course of his commercial dealings. During his stay there, he observed that all the town's Jews often spoke in very high praise of the exceeding saintliness and wisdom of the Hasidic rebbe, the Maggid Dov Be'er of Mezhirech.

It, therefore, became fixed in his mind that he must call on this Rabbi and examine the veracity of this talk. Although not gifted with Torah learning, he was a G-d fearing man. By habit, however, he was not inclined to the approach of the hasidic rebbes. For this reason he wished to hear words of Torah from the Maggid himself and to ask him this and that of wondrous matters. Then he would consider in his heart if the Maggid spoke truth.

As so it was. He was ushered into the presence of the Maggid and received the traditional Jewish blessing "Shalom, peace be unto you". Then, without any preliminary words, the Maggid declared,

- Know my son that it is not the remedy administered to the patient by the physician which heals, but rather the physician himself. For each physician there is a heavenly mediator betwixt himself and the Almighty, an astral angel through which the Lord of the Universe casts his great light upon him. It is this luminary which empowers the physician to heal, and he must learn to use this power for the good. The medications administered are superficial, only that which has been exposed to our eye.

- However, the greatest physician is accompanied by the arch-Angel Rafael himself who heals the patient with his own transcendent power.

The Maggid spoke no more to this man who was very amazed, and thought to himself, "Well, I am not a physician, nor was my father a physician, and what has the Maggid said to me?"

Since he knew not how to judge these matters, the words of the rebbe seemed falacious. Again he reviewed them in his mind. Perhaps it was an allegory? But still he was not able to fathom their meaning and so departed the rebbe's house, convinced that they were of no importance. He continued his business travels, journeying along his prescribed route for an additional three months time before he finally returned home.

Soon after his return he was taken very ill. The doctors came and went, but to no avail. Indeed, the man's life was on the wane and from day to day it seemed to be drawing to an end.

Because he was a wealthy and well-known notable of Vilna, the townspeople were in an uproar and took great pains each to bring his own physician. But the physicians were of no benefit to the sick man and no help at all. He had already lost the strength to speak and all could see that he was at death's door. Then the townspeople raised their voices in prayer and in a great surge of weeping. There was tumult and the clamor of Psalm-reading in all the batei-midrash and batei knesset for this important patrician of the

Jewish community, that he might recover from his mysterious ailment.

Several persons, of greater and lesser importance, had gathered at the sick bed so that the dying man should not be alone at the time his soul would depart his material body. And since the house was not large enough to hold all those who wished to be there, a great crowd had extended into the street outside the entrance to this house.

At that hour, a turbulence arose from the roadway. The King of Prussia himself was passing. When the people learned of this, it occurred to them to request an audience with the king and beg that the king's personal physician might be permitted to attend the ailing man, for it was well known that the king always travelled with his personal physician.

And this is what they did. The Jewish patricians and notables of Vilna went to the hospice of the King of Prussia and there appealed to him that he might dispatch his personal physician to attend their neighbor who was so ill. He agreed and the physician was immediately sent to the home of the dying man. The contingent of notables followed him into the house, and behind them were all the people, so that the house was crowded from window to door.

When the physician saw that he had come there to treat a man who was almost dead he was very angry,

- Why have you called me to heal a man at death's door? Can I waken the dead?

This is what he said, and he turned to leave the house. But, by virtue of the many people who had crowded the house and left no possible exit, he was unable to depart. He pressed himself forward to leave, but the crowd did not disperse. In this way he was delayed for ten minutes, when, suddenly glancing at the face of the dying man, he saw an improvement. Approaching the bed, he laid his hands upon him. Seeing there was some hope, he raised his voice and insisted that the crowd disperse so that their presence would not confuse him. Now, they attended to his wish. They moved aside and began to depart from the house.

He thought to himself,

- I can see now that there is some hope.

Sitting down he wrote out instructions for a medicinal remedy which he dispatched to the apothocery, waiting there to see what would be the effect of his curative potion.

As he sat to await the remedy, he watched the face of the patient. What was this? There was an even greater improvement! Now the patient was in need of a different potion. He wrote a second note to be sent off in place of the first. However, after the second remedy had been sent for he glanced again at the face of the patient and what did he see? A further improvement! Moment by moment, the course of this man's illness was being reversed.

Astonished, the physician thought deeply about this strange disease. Concerned that he might appear to be an ignorant and inexperienced physician who did not understand what medication was needed by a patient, he instructed those attending the man that there was no longer need of the curatives which he had requested from the apothecary.

The messengers returned bearing the medications; these the physician placed in his bag. He was astounded at what he had witnessed, never having heard of such an incident during his long career. Lingering at the man's side, he pondered for a while. Was this some new kind of illness which he had never seen?

Soon the patient sat up in his bed. Taking hold of the doctor's hand, he said to him,

- Please sir, tarry yet a while, for I have something to say to you . . . During my travels this year a great rebbe told me the following,

- "Each physician is accompanied by an astral angel

166

through which the Lord of the Universe casts his great light upon him. It is this luminary which empowers the physician to heal and he must learn to use this power for the good. However, the greatest doctor is accompanied by the arch-Angel Rafael who heals the sick by his own power."

The patient continued to implore,

- I appeal to you to remain with me for another short while, for I see that the words of the rebbe to me were truth and this is why I have recovered without the agency of medication. My soul observed you from the time you entered my home until this very moment. I have been breathing in new life. Blessed is the Almighty, you are that great physician and I am well without curative potions.

When the doctor heard these words, he was even more surprised and he weighed them seriously in his mind for he was a superior and a very wise physician. Then he asked the patient,

- And who is the rabbi who told you these things?

- Truth to tell, I did not understand then what he meant to say to me and so his words seemed false. I was travelling through a town in Poland called Mezhirech. There I heard tell of a Gaon, the holy Maggid Rebbe Dov Be'er. My heart could not believe the rumor of his greatness and therefore I went myself to scrutinize this vessel. Immediately when I entered his presence, he said to me what I have told you now about physicians. Today, I recall his words. They have been my destiny, and so it seems to me that the utterances of the Almighty are on his lips. They are true from beginning to end.

The physician replied,

- I can see that you speak the truth. This rabbi is a very wise man who speaks prophecy.

The physician then wrote down the name of the city and of the Maggid Rebbe Dov Be'er. He composed a new apothecary note to hasten recuperation, and thanking the patient for enriching him with these matters, he bid him farewell.

The physician returned home with the King's entourage. He was quite agitated and ferment had taken hold of his heart as a result of the things he had lately witnessed and heard, for he was a Jewish man. Being the King's physician, he had not been observant of the precepts of Judaism. He had also fallen deeply into weaknesses of sensual lust, and a party of his favorite female companions accompanied him on all his travels.

However, his experience in Vilna caused him to decide to embark on a journey and to see this Maggid Rebbe for himself. Since he could not abandon the King without his physician, upon returning home he thanked the King and asked for a letter of release. In preparation for the journey, he arranged for a magnificent coach for himself and his beloved ladies who accompanied him.

Along the road, he began to ponder and consider his behavior. What he was doing? Travelling to the saintly Maggid accompanied by his lady friends!

Convinced that he must separate himself, with difficulty he parted from them one by one; and as he neared the town of Mezhirech he sold his magnificent coach and the horses.

Each day of his journey, his heart instructed that he shed another sensual lust. And, as they say, the heavenly powers come to the aid of he who wishes to cleanse himself. Thus, along his route to the Maggid Rebbe the physician's soul was unfolding and he became a different man.

Finally arriving in the town of Mezhirech, he went directly to the house of the Rabbi Dov Be'er.

When Rabbi Dov-Be'er saw the physician, without preamble he said to him,

- I have awaited and anticipated you this long time. Now I will be the physician of your soul and you will be the physician of my body.

The physician, who remained with the Maggid a very long time, came to be a great and learned zaddik. For he was a truely wise man whose primary soul had been of the highest level. It had fallen into the deepest recesses when his corporeal shell succumbed to the sensual desires of this world and allowed these to rule him.

In this way the Rabbi Maggid raised him from the depths and helped him to surmount his weakness. The physician's soul was returned to the vital quarry from which it had been hewn, and reunited with his superior and pristine spirit.

Ritual Objects

You Have Graced Man with Understanding

I n his early years, Rabbi Shmelke of Nicholsburg had a dear friend, a youth of very keen intellect. When he grew to be a man, this devout prodigy was taken on as the Presiding Judge of the Bet-Din and Rav of the city of Ya-nuh.

His childhood comrade grew into a faithful Torah scholar who was observant of all the mitzvot, and all his flock honored him and took example from his holy ways. The one drawback was perhaps that he was by nature very obstinate. Never in his life did he relinquish his own opinion to any other person's in this world.

The years went by, and the Rabbi of Ya'nuh arranged a marraige between his first-born son and the daughter of a rabbi from a distant town. When it was time for the marriage, he invited the Torah scholars and the notables of his community to honor him by accompanying himself and the bridegroom on their journey to the wedding.

Thus did they journey in fine harnessed carriages to enhance the rabbi's honor. As for the rabbi, he sat high in a most elegant carriage alongside the gifted and well versed bridegroom. And one young gentleman yeshiva student joined them to occupy the bridegroom with words of Torah along his mitzvah journey, so that no time be wasted in idle matters.

Soon it was the minchah hour and the rabbi and his entourage descended from the carriage in order to perform their ministrations in preparation for the minchah prayer. The rabbi, as was his habit, went off by himself to a tree in the wood, to make ready in private and to cleanse himself for prayer.

All returned to the carriage to wait for their rabbi, but he did not join them. The sun set and still the rabbi tarried. Wondering greatly, the groom, the head of the community and the yeshiva student went to search for their rabbi in the forest; perhaps he had extended his prayers. And they did not succeed in finding him.

Considerably alarmed, for darkness now enveloped the land, they returned to the king's road where the carriages waited. Several smaller wagons also traveling to the wedding came up beside them.

- Why has the rabbi's party delayed on the road?, these people asked.

- The rabbi has gone into the wood and now cannot be found.

- We think it likely that the notable gevir of our city, who is traveling alone to the wedding, saw the rabbi standing in the forest and has taken him in his carraige. Surely they have gone on ahead together.

Hearing this, all agreed that this must be so and they left that place. Nevertheless, all along their route, they searched and asked other travelers about their rabbi, but everyone said that surely he had gone on ahead in the carraige of the gevir.

Now, when they arrived at the city where the wedding was

to be held and learned that the rabbi, the father of the groom, had not arrived, they grew very sad. Some people thought that he had returned home by foot after losing his way in the forest, or perhaps he stopped a passing wagon. In that way, he at least would not lose time in not learning Torah, since he well knew that the wedding would take place with or without him.

The conclusion was that the wedding was held under a melancholy cloud which lay heavy on both families. After the wedding feast was over, the householders from Ya-nuh traveled home and all along their way they asked everyone whether they had seen Rabbenu. And all replied, "No. We have no knowledge of him."

And when they arrived home, envoys were dispatched to each and every city in the region to seek after their rabbi, but for a long time all their toil was fruitless.

As for the rabbi, it happened that when he had wished to leave the forest and return to the straight road, he lost his direction and his feet took paths winding among the great trees. In this way, he wandered several parasangs deeper into the great tangle of forest. All that night he walked farther and farther into the forest and found no way out. When the sun rose beyond the trees, he stopped to rest a while and to recite the "Shemah Yisrael" prayer, and was forced to complete his prayers without his prayer shawl and tefillin, which had remained in the carriage with his baggage.

He continued to circle round the forest for many days and did not find his way out. Satisfing his hunger with fruits of the forest, when he felt worn and spent he laid down to rest on the soft forest floor.

And the day came that, because of all his trouble, weariness and worry, he lost count of the days of the week and erred regarding the Sabbath, for he had lost one weekday in his reckoning. In other words, he was now certain that the sixth day of the week, which was Friday the eve of the holy Shabbos, was instead the Shabbos itself. This caused him to sanctify the sixth day, in place of the seventh, with all the holiness and splendor which he could assemble in the forest.

And the blessed Almighty watched over him that no evil befall him, by virtue of his Torah learning and his good works.

After many days had passed, the Rabbi of Ya-nuh emerged from the forest and came to a place of habitation where he was told of his location. Burdened with his adventures, he returned to his city and his home, where he related all that had befallen him to the family.

That day was the fifth day of Sabbath week and before evening fell the Rabbi began to prepare himself to welcome the sacred Shabbos Queen. He wondered greatly why all his household was not likewise occupied in preparation for the holy day which was almost upon them, but they responded by explained that he had erred in his reckoning since that day was only Thursday.

Now the rabbi, during the trial and tribulation of his forced isolation in the forest, had fallen into a black melancholy and had become a kind of "fool about a particular matter". He was convinced without a doubt that his reckoning was correct and that the members of his household, and, indeed all the Jews of the town, were mistaken. The arguments and logic presented before him to repair his error were of no use. It was not possible to free him from his mind-set that the fifth day of the week was the sixth, and Shabbos eve.

Everyone now became convinced that the rabbi was no longer balanced in his mind, and this caused his family to fall into a great gloom. But what could they do about it? They had no choice but to prepare a Shabbat feast for him and as the night of Friday eve descended, the rabbi went to the bet knesset and there welcomed the Shekhinah with great joy, as though it were Shabbos eve. The townspeople laughed behind his back, amused at the unfortunate man's strange madness. Nevertheless, the rabbi honored the day according to his own reckoning and with great splendor. He recited the Torah portion and said the special thanksgiving blessing for one whose life has been saved.

The next morning, which was Friday and which he considered to be Shabbos, the rabbi did not put on his tefillin, since a man is forbidden to do so on this day.

In the afternoon, when he saw all the members of his household beginning preparations to welcome the Sabbath Queen, he grew very angry with them. And on the next day when the holy Shabbos was being observed by all the Jews of the world, the rabbi put on his tefillin and performed labor. Thus, the joy which had re-entered his household when he was found now turned to melancholy and mourning.

Several weeks passed and no one could change the rabbi's mind and convince him of his error. Both local rabbis and the great personages of Israel came to speak to him, pleading that he abandon this mistake. They spoke long and presented signs and proof that he had lost a day in calculating the week while wandering in the forest.

However, as we have said, he was by nature an unusually obstinate man and had become unbalanced in his mind in this particular matter, although in all other things he was as reasonable as any other man. Clinging firm and obstinate to his mistake, he persevered like a pitiful fool and rejected their logic.

Soon, word of this tale reached his boyhood friend, Rabbenu Reb' Shmelke, Shmuel Horovitz, who was at that time the Presiding Judge of the Beit Din of the Shinova community. He set out on a journey to his friend, arriving on the fifth day of Sabbath week – which according to the reckoning of the Rabbi of Ya-nuh was the sixth day, the eve of the Shabbos. Affectionately and with joy they greeted

175

each other, renewing their loyal boyhood ties. The Rabbi of Ya-nuh invited Reb' Smelke to be his guest, and he replied,

- This is exactly the purpose of my visit.

Reb' Shmelke dropped a hint to the householders of Ya-nuh that they begin to ready themselves in the accustomed manner, as if for the Sabbath, according to the reckoning of their rabbi. And that they bring out the well aged, rich wine. After the noon hour all went to the ritual bath, and as evening fell they put on their Sabbath finery and went to pray together with their rabbi.

In their hearts, the townspeople dreaded that Reb' Shmelke might have been caught up, the Almighty forbid it, in their rabbi's error and was now sharing his mistaken calculation of the days of the week. But at the synagogue, Reb' Shmelke left the honor of conducting "Shabbos" prayers to their Rabbi, while he, together with the rest of the congregation, prayed the correct, weekday prayer. Then the congregation went to their homes in peace and joy as is the custom.

Many congregants accompanied the two friends to the house of the rabbi, extending their respect to the honorable guest Reb' Shmelke, and singing, "Shalom Aleichem" to the Shabbos Queen in joyous nigun. Reciting the blessing over the wine, all sat down to the "Shabbos meal", exchanging enlightening words of learning and Torah.

Rabbi Shmelke suggested to his boyhood friend that that they conduct the meal as a celebratory feast in order to give thanks to the Almighty for the miracle of the rabbi's return to his home alive and well. Rabbi Shmelke hinted that the Rabbi be served the rich and well aged wine which had been set out on the table. This wine was well known to be very intoxicating, and always caused the drinker to fall into a deep slumber. Rabbi Shmelke encouraged his friend to drink and to drink again, all the while speaking words of praise and gratitude to the Lord of the Universe. And so it was.

The Rabbi of Ya-nuh fell into a deep sleep at the table. Then Rabbi Shmelke indicated that the family place a pillow beneath the rabbi's head and allow him to sleep comfortably. Then he took up his pipe and enjoyed a good smoke, after which he adressed the company seated there,

- Now. You can all go about your every day business, each and every one of you. Conduct your work affairs and your commerce. Soon, with the help of the Blessed One Be His Name, all will fall into place.

And he instructed them that all those present return to the house of the rabbi on the following night, which would truly be the holy Shabbat.

- At the very same time and hour, you will take up the positions that you hold now.

Rabbi Shmelke himself sat at the table all that night and all through the following day, keeping watch that no one waken his friend. And indeed, the Rabbi slept deeply through Friday.

Soon it was Shabbos eve. Rabbi Shmelke did not go to bet knesset. He chanted the Shabbos eve prayers alone in the house of his friend and was faithful at his side. Then the congregation began to return for the festive meal. They sat themselves in the same seats as the evening before. And the Rabbi of Ya-nuh slept still.

Rabbi Shmelke enjoyed the true Sabbath meal, in happy contentment. Then he favored the table and all those gathered around him with heartfelt words of Torah, until it was the midnight hour. Only then did the Rabbi ofYa-nuh awaken from his slumber.

His friend said to him,

- Awake and rise from your sleep. We are readying now to recite the birkat hamazon, the blessing of thanks and grace for our food.

Waking from his long sleep, the rabbi looked around him at those present, then said to his friend,

- It appears to me that I have overdone the wine and slept too long.

Rising, he washed his hands in the ritual manner, and after granting sagacious comments of Torah to the company gathered at his table, he joined them in the thanksgiving grace after the meal.

Until the day of his passing, the Rabbi of Ya-nuh did not know what had taken place. To the contrary, he praised himself that all had admitted to his judgment and now sanctified the holy Shabbos according to his reckoning. He was always very grateful to his dear friend for standing by him and convincing his household and the entire Jewish community of his city as to their error, and that his opinion was just.

And he believed this all the days of his life.

Rabbi Reb' Shmelke, who proved himself wise in profound matters of the soul, decreed that all the people of this town must never reveal their rabbi's mistake and they must never speak of it again.

For a bribe blinds the eyes of the wise

A true story of Rabbi Abraham Yehoshua Heschel of Aphta at the time that he served as Av Bet Din of the city of Kolvishuv. And this was prior to his service as rabbi to the cities of Aphta, Jassy and Medzibezh. Once, he presided over an important law suit jointly with several other dayyanim. Now, unknown to him, his fellow judges had accepted a bribe from a certain wealthy man who was a litigant in this suit, for they intended to miscarry justice and to find the wealthy man not liable.

And Rabbi Abraham Yehoshua Heschel opposed his colleagues in their decision since it negated the halachic ruling.

These judges of the Torah court advised the wealthy litigant to bribe their fellow judge, Rabbi Heschel. But the man was certain that this would not be possible, since Rabbi Abraham Yehoshua Heschel was known to be a true zaddik. A scheme, therefore, was devised by his advisors wherein the litigant would secret a large amount of gold coins in the rabbi's special Rosh Chodesh coat – which he wore only on the celebratory first day of each Hebrew month. So, this is what he did, and the rabbi knew nothing of the deception.

After this, when Rabbi Heschel once again sat with his

colleague judges to determine the ruling, inexplicably he began to observe that his opinion was changing and now tending toward their own. This caused him to ask for a delay,

- We will decide the ruling in the morning.

Thus said, he departed to his chamber. There he fell to weeping, and imploring the Blessed One Be His Name to help him understand why his original, true judgement had suddenly altered in his mind.

- Why do I now agree with the unjust determination of the other judges? For the truths of the Torah instruct me that their decision is not suited to halachic law, which is our canon in these matters.

He postponed the litigation one day and then another. Thus, for several days he did not disclose his opinion. On the day that Rosh Chodesh was upon him, he removed his special coat from the closet to wear for the occasion. When he donned the coat, it seemed unusually weighty. Casting his hand into the coat pocket, he found it laden with gold coins. Consulting with his wife, he asked,

- Who has been in my chamber and secreted all these gold coins in my coat pocket?

They considered the matter and soon it became clear that the gevir who was now a litigator before the court, had placed the gold coins there. The rabbi sent for the gevir and proscribed a ban upon him until he would confess. When he admitted his crime, Rabbi Heschel returned his money, admonishing him,

- Leave this place, you evil man. By your cause I have been disqualified from sitting in judgment in my court.

And Rabbi Avraham Yehoshua Heschel of Aphta was wont to say that this was the intention of the Torah verse which states, "A bribe blinds the eyes of the wise and perverts the words of the righteous."

For, even if the bribe is presented to a pure zaddik, and

180

though it is delivered without the zaddik's knowledge, judgement will be distorted.

THE GATES OF REPENTANCE

Thy Children Shall Return To Their Own Border

I
n the days that Rabbi Abraham Yehoshua Heschel of Aphta, the author of "Ohav Yisrael" - "He Who Loves Israel" - had not yet been revealed as Gaon and Zaddik, he served as the Rabbi of the city of Kolvishuv in Poland. It was with great difficulty that he eked out a living for himself and his household.

The Dukes of Poland were sovereign monarchs in their individual provinces, but were obligated to pay a tax to their King Pontovski, whose throne sat in the city of Warsaw. Every three years they journeyed to the King's court to consult in assembly and make decisions for the good of the state. Then each would return home to his duchy.

Kolvishuv was situated in the province of a certain Grand Duke whose manor house was a distance of several parasangs from the city. Many other cities and towns were under the control of this most important Duke whose high station afforded him leadership over all the nobles assembled in Warsaw. Indeed, his seat was next to the king. And he was a great Jew hater. No man of Israel conducting his business in the court of this Duke had ever seen his face, for only the manor stewards dealt with them.

One time, an upstanding Jew of handsome countenance came to the court to market grain, and the language of Poland was fine on his lips. This Jew came from a small town in that province, and he only had a bit of ma'ot in his pocket. The first time he approached the steward, that one was pleased with his appearance and refined way of speech. Thereupon, the steward said to the Jew,

- If you trade with me regularly, I will extend you several hundred rubels worth of grain on credit.

This arrangement held good for a short time. The Jew bought grain in the value of several hundred rubels, and the steward's custom was to extend him credit for the grain for longer than was usual. The steward did this without his lord's knowledge. Until one day the Duke died.

After a time, when the Jew came as usual to the steward's quarters to conduct his business, the Duchess was watching from a distance and she could see how very handsome he was. Sending immediately for the steward, she asked,

- Who is that person?

- This man is an honest Jew who is also very reliable in business matters.

- When he completes affairs at your house, send him to me.

The steward returned to say that the Duchess wished the Jew to call upon her at the manor house. At this, the Jewish merchant became very alarmed, but was reassured by the steward,

- Do not fear at all, for it appears that you have found favor in her eyes.

At the manor house, the Duchess received her guest with great courtesy, and inquired,

- From what city do you come; and what is your business here?

He trembled at the honor she had extended him. And soon he began to come and go at the manor house at her invitation. And so it went, until familiarity caused the Duchess to reveal her love and demand that he marry her, saying,

- My property will become yours, and you will enjoy all the honors extended my first husband; his ministerial post at Warsaw and all his privileges in the state of Poland.

At first he was somewhat doleful at the circumstance in which he found himself. But the Duchess did not waver from her pleas, imploring exceedingly that he convert to her faith and become the recipient of much wealth and honor.

The day came that he succumbed and promised to follow her wishes. They agreed that within two weeks time she was to dispatch two servants to his home who would accompany him to her house where two Polish priests would convert him to her faith. He would change his name to that of her late husband, the Duke. And the Duchess gave him two hundred gold coins, that he might leave the money with his wife when abandoning her.

The Jew traveled home and after the alloted time had passed two servants came to call for him. He locked the two hundred gold coins away in the table drawer, together with a letter to his wife. Although he gave his wife the key, he did not reveal the truth to her and only said that he was going away on a business journey.

And so he joined the Duchess, converted from his own faith and soon was a hater of Israel. The Duchess loved him greatly and with time bore him three children.

Three years passed and time came for all the dukes to journey to the governing assembly at the court of the King in Warsaw, as did the new Duke. At the feast he was seated next to King Ponivotski, as was fitting for the most Grand Duke whose name he had taken on. His handsome countenance, tall stature and fine manner of speech found much favor in the eyes of the King. Thus, he extended his stay in Warsaw for several weeks, and each day, seated at the King's table, he was afforded the place of honor due his superior rank.

The day came that one of the Dukes seated at the king's table related the following incident which he claimed had taken place in his village.

- Close to the time that the Hebrews celebrate their festival of the matzah, Passover, a young Jewish girl took a local gentile girl for a walk not far from the village. The Jewish girl later returned to the village alone. The gentile girl never returned, until this very day. For the Jews slaughtered her and drew her blood, since they have need of gentile blood to prepare their Passover holiday.

This is what he related. And all the other nobles seated there agreed, nodding their heads before the King,

- This is a very well known fact, what is new about it? In our towns and cities we well know the fact that each and every year before the Passover holiday the Jews capture several gentile souls, because they have need to steal their blood for the Passover.

When the King heard this, he was furious at the Jews and his anger burned within him. He questioned all seated there as to the truth of this accusation, and they all replied as one voice,

- This is the truth, the Jews are extreme murderers.

At this, King Ponitovski decreed that no Jew would remain in Poland and all their property would be taken from them. He commanded that a written judgment be drawn up, and every man there must witness and sign it, from the lowest ranking until the highest ranking noble. And the King signed last, as was the law in Poland.

The new Grand Duke, who had converted and abandoned his Judaism, heard the claims of all the other Dukes and was silent. But now, when he must sign this

Seder Night

document with his own hand, a pure thought of sacred worth was aroused in him. For prior to abandoning his faith he had been a scholar of Torah. Now his soul revived the holy knowledge in him, and in his heart he considered, "There is a saying of our late sages, 'He who saves the life of one man in Israel, it is as if he saved the entire world.' Therefore, the act is manifold if I save the whole of Israel!"

For even though he was sunken into the basest of defilements, the Jewish Grand Duke could not bear to listen to this libel which had resounded at the Council of Dukes. Trembling, and overtaken with a terrible agitation, he rose from his seat in fury. His voice was raised high and he spoke out in superb wisdom,

- Listen to my words, for I speak today of my own sin. . . I was once a Jew. And who can know better than myself of Jewish evil and the malice of their hearts. But this thing of which you tell, that the Jews have need of blood for Passover – and all the nobles present here each related a story to prove this – that is a lie, a foolish tale and a vain deception. I can guarantee that what I say is the truth. What is more, a severe prohibition is written into the Torah which the Jews must obey against eating blood, even of animals. I know accurately that this tale is entirely deception and falsehood, and I will not sign false witness before the king.

Then the King asked him,

- Can you say this for certain, that the Jews have never performed such an act?

The Jewish convert replied to the king in a strong voice,

- It is a total lie and I can guarantee it.

The King turned to all the company seated there and vented his disdain and humiliation on them for deceiving him. He then cancelled the harsh edict and tore up the document containing all the signatures.

The time came for the Dukes to return to their homes. And this man who had risen to defend all of Israel, was now granted Divine Providence for his act. Holy ideas were aroused within him, that he might be raised from his level of defilement. He began to long for repentance, to once again carry out the precepts of the Jewish faith with love. His soul in turmoil, he cast himself about in despair as one mad or lunatic. On the journey home, he no longer felt the emotion of love for the Duchess or for his sons that she had borne him.

The Duchess, however, who loved him with a strong and exceptional love and anticipated her husband's homecoming anxiously, greeted him with words of ardour and affection upon his return from Warsaw. Although he now felt only repulsion towards her, he did not reveal the secrets of his heart, but wandered to and fro as one who has lost his way, or taken leave of his senses.

Seeing that his heart was bereft of joy, the Duchess advised her husband to embark on a restful journey to the forest region. There he could walk the meadows and watch the ordinary folk going about their everyday affairs; one reaps his field and the other plants, this one builds and the other tears down. Such occupation might calm his senses, since surely he had become overly wearied in Warsaw.

The thought of a journey appealed greatly to him because he wanted to put a distance between himself and his wife, so as not to see her face. Harnessing fine team of horses and carriage, he traveled to the city of Kolvishuv. There he tied up the team and carriage at the outskirts of the city, and entered astride a single horse, his best stick in hand, in the conceit of Polish ministers. It was after the midnight hour. Knocking on the door of a hostelry, he was welcomed by the owner who put the horse up in his stable. He then asked the owner of the hostel to point out the house of the rabbi of the city of Kolvishuv.

Walking stick in hand, the convert approached the house of Rabbi Abraham Yehoshua Heshel of Aphta, of holy blessed memory. All the household was asleep, and only the rebbe was awake, since it was his habit to recite the "Tikkun Hazot" during the midnight watch.

Confronted by a man in the custume of a Polish minister, Rabbi Abraham Yehoshua Heshel asked,

- Who are you?

- I am the well-known Grand Duke who was a Jew and who abandoned his faith. Now I wish to again adhere to the foundation stone from which I was hewn. I long to return to the religion of Israel.

And he told the rebbe nothing of what had transpired in Warsaw. He continued,

- Therefore, I inquired and sought after a great Rabbi Hahkam among the Jews, an important man of Torah. I was told that in this very city of Kolvishuv, there resides a scholar of exceptional learning and wisdom. This is why I have come here, to benefit from your advice; to hear from your lips how I can repent and rejoin the religion of Israel.

Rabbi Abraham Yehoshua Heshel did not wish to speak to him at all because he was very frightened that this man might bring harm and be caused to bear false witness against the Israelites if the matter became known. For surely the Duchess would search after her husband. The rebbe walked up and down the rooms of his house and asked only to be left to himself and that the man leave. He refused to exchange another word with him. But the Grand Duke did not cease his pleas for pity and for advice as to how to return to the faith of his fathers.

Noting his own walking stick poised upright in the corner of his room, Rabbi Abraham Yehoshua Heshel made a vow.

- When I see grass of the field flowering from my stick, I will speak to you and instruct you.

Still the Duke stood before him in supplication as petitioner, that the rebbe might take pity on him. After a while, the rebbe looked over at his walking stick and behold!

Grass of the field was sprouting forth from the dry wood. Recognizing a true sign from the Almighty, the rebbe became alarmed. Composing himself, he asked the man to tell his tale from begining to end. When he had related everything that had happened to him and what he had told the King at the assembly in Warsaw, it was clear to the rebbe that this meritorious act of saving Israel had aroused the man to repentence. Divine Providence now prompted him to purify all his sins.

So Rabbi Abraham Yehoshua Heshel advised him how he might escape his situation and return to his people,

- Journey to the city of Amsterdam. I will give you a letter for the Rabbi of Amsterdam, who will reach out both arms to embrace and protect you. And I too will pray that your soul is healed.

The Duke thanked the rabbi for this blessing, his countenance bright with joy of release. The rabbi accompanied him to the hostelry and returned home and no man knew of these matters.

The Duke was admitted to the hostel and immediately set out again astride his horse. Beyond the city limits, he joined his team and carriage and journeyed back to the Duchess. But he was sickened and could not look her in the face. Seeing that his reason had not returned to him, and that he would not smile upon her, she became very bitter and lost all desire to live. Then she advised him thus,

- There is one friend who for a long time now has been asking that you visit with him, and pass the time. Since your heart is unsettled in you, go and travel to this gentleman. Would that you sweeten this gall of your heart and enjoy your stay with him.

This proposal appeared good since it offered an opportunity to escape. He immediately instructed that a suitable conveyance be made ready. He took with him only costs for the journey for he did not want to enjoy the Duchesses' money any longer.

When he arrived at the border of Poland, he left the carriage and the horses with the coachman. One horse carried him over the border, and no man knew his destination. From there, he fled to the city of Amsterdam, where he presented the letter of Rabbi Abraham Yehoshua Heschel, of blessed memory, to the Chief Rabbi, who welcomed him with hospitality, and there he rested.

After a long time had passed, a letter arrived from the Rabbi of Kolvishov informing him that his bigamous marriage was declared nul and void. And Rabbi Heschel instructed that in his prayers he must do penitance for his soul. And the rabbi of the city of Amsterdam gave his blessing, that he may return to his first home, and to his wife.

This is how a Jew who abandoned his faith saved his people and returned to them. And he was a perfect zaddik until the day of his death.

Protector of
Orphans
and the Poor

O nce, after the holy Shabbos Queen had departed from us and the commonplace passage of week days resumed, the Ba'al Shem Tov set forth in his carriage, as was his wont. Three of his most excellent students accompanied him on that evening, and although in actuality they had traveled only several parasangs, by virtue of the Besh't's holy state, their carriage and its passengers achieved a far distance.

When the second day of that Sabbath week came upon them they had lost their way, and were wandering in a barren desert where they found no habitation or town. The thoughts of the Baal Shem Tov became undone and he was perplexed as to why he had been thus overcome.

They traveled on for three days, until they found themselves in a maze of forest where they did not recognize day or night. And so it was until the sixth day, the eve of the Shabbos. Weary and forlorn, where could they rest and observe the holy day? The great wisdom of the Besh't had abandoned him and his mind was as a simple man; and for this reason his students were even more dismayed.

Observing that it was Shabbos eve, and that still they had not arrived at their destination, the Besh't in his anguish, and with distress and groaning, fell into a slumber. Suddenly, at the noon hour of that day, the face of the universe turned bright and from afar a shining came to them like day-light. Joyous at this sign, all said,

- Blessed be He, and blessed His name, since surely now we arrive at an inhabited town. Surely the holy day will not come upon our senses as a confusion.

This gleaming shone forth before them like the sun, drawing them to the source of this luminescence – it was a house at a distance.

Soon they approached the small house within the forest clearing where a coarse-featured Jewish man, dressed as a simpleton, and with bare feet was standing at the door. The Besh't's party drew close and asked if it would be possible to rest in his house on the holy Shabbos.

He replied,

- I do not wish you to stay here because I can see by your faces that you are counted among the hasidim and maggidim. For many years now I have hated such people, even as my mother and father hated such people. Therefore, continue on your way, since I do not even wish to look at your faces.

Thus he ridiculed and scorned them. Then they asked,

- Is there a settlement nearby where we can stay?

- There is such a place, but it is very distant.

Imploring that he might allow them to enter his house for the Sabbath, the party offered to pay much money for their food and drink. Finally he agreed, but only on a double and triple condition: that they not pray out loud, as was their manner, so as not to frighten the gentile neighbors; that they do not exercise the hasidic habit of deep forethought and

196

long preparations for their prayer, for he was a hungry man and must eat right away, morning and evening; and that they not examine the food carefully to be assured that it is kosher according to the hasidic custom. To all these three conditions they were forced to agree and say "Amen".

Entering the house and resting a bit from the trials and travails of the road, the Besh't asked their host whether there was a flowing river or a natural spring nearby, so that they could immerse and cleanse themselves in honor of the Shabbos. When the man heard the Besh't's words, he began to curse and make many bellicose remarks, complaining that he was certain and could prove that they were thieves. In a fury, he threatened to take all their belongings and throw them out the door. So they implored and beseeched him with many words of peace until he abandoned his anger and once again permitted them into his house.

They wondered greatly at this man, since they had never seen such a coarse and dirty person in all their days. Furthermore, in his home there were no possessions, no table or stool, except for four support posts inserted into the earth and on top of which were laid a square section of board. The rooms were unoccupied or closed off, appearing to be in ruins. All this was confusion to them. Neither fowl nor feline shared his roof, only he alone dwelt there.

These things caused a dread to take hold of them. The sun moved forward on its path and still they witnessed no preparations for the festive meals. He only paced from corner to corner and chewed on the raw fruit of the land, whistling in the habit of the gentile folk. Each to the other wondered if perhaps the man was not even a Shabbos observer as was befitting a Jew.

When the day turned, this man covered his table with a heavy black linen rag. He tossed a piece of black loam onto the rag and poking a hole in it with his finger, pushed one small candle into the loam which he lit. The Besh't's party

Ecstasy of Chassidic dance

saw all these things and became more frightened. They had not seen him pray the mincha prayer, but instead he began the Friday night table ritual without prelude, quickly gulping down all the syllables and words of the prayer, as the ignorant folk do. He bent this way and that and already his prayer was finished. Thus, they were also forced to shorten their prayers, according to the conditions that he had laid down for them.

Nevertheless, they greeted him,

- Good Shabbos.

But he replied,

- May you have an evil Shabbos.

When they wanted to sing the piyut "Shalom Aleichem" – "Welcome Celestial Host" – he silenced them angrily with shameful murmurings and blasphemy. Then, taking up his glass and again swallowing the syllables and missing entire words, he chanted the kiddush blessing over the wine, but not before he declared that his blessing would have serve all present in this mitzvah. They pleaded with him that he allow them to recite their own kiddush over the wine, and on the weekday they would pay him much money for this indulgence. But he did not allow it under any circumstances, claiming that very soon the lone candle would be extinguished, and time pressed.

After the blessing, he yawned his mouth open wide and gulped down the entire cup of wine and because only the smallest drop remained in the bottom of the glass, they were prevented from sharing in his kiddush blessing. He mocked them,

- Drunkards!. . . Don't drink too much.

He lay a heavy slice of black bread on the table and when they asked to fulfill the mitzvah of two loaves, he gaped open his mouth without measure and was ready to swallow them alive. Too, the cup for ritual cleansing of hands before bread was flawed, but what could they do against this man's will? He had set down his conditions and they had accepted.

Knowing well that among the hasidim each man held the blessing loaf before the slicing, he did not permit them to touch the loaf, saying that their hands were dirty and had been up to mischief. He cut a slice for himself and handed each a morsel. Thus, they were forced to bend to his evil ways. He brought lentile porridge and giant spoons like shovels to the table, saying,

- Eat!

Head bent over the bowl, he ate as gluttons do, without glancing at his guests. In addition, he did not permit words of Torah at his table and they had to whisper the blessing after food each to himself. The end of it was a confusion of their senses, so much so that they did not know if it was Shabbos eve or some other day of the week.

After this, he gave to the Besh't an article of women's clothing to place under his head and to Rabbi David Pirkas, the Besh't's eminent student, who wrote the chronicles of this tale down, he gave a forbidden piece of shatnez fabric, wool woven together with linen, which gentiles are accustomed to sleep in. They refused to accept these things from him, and he mocked and cursed them abundantly.

Before the light of the Sabbath day, this man was already walking about barefoot in his home, singing his prayers very quickly and to a gentile tavern tune. Against their will, the Besh't and his students began to rush themselves so as to complete prayers with him. This caused them even more pain than they had experienced on the Sabbath eve. And after the minchah prayer, when they longed to perform the mitzvah of the se'uda shlishit, he refused to give them food at all, saying,

- Gluttons and drunkards all! You have just eaten! Now you wish to eat again? It is as Moses said of the Children of

Israel who hungered in the desert "Shall flocks and herds be slain for them, to suffice them?"

Forced to conduct the third Shabbos meal with only words of Torah secretly spoken, the Besh't and his students felt themselves emptied of the brilliant wisdom of their minds, and bereft of their exceptional achievements. And they knew nothing of why and wherefore this experience had fallen upon them.

Evening came, and their host said,

- Must I serve you another meal this evening?

They thought in their hearts that this man could eat his coarse meal by himself. They would only partake of a morsel, for the purpose of the melave malka mitzvah. Too this repast was laden with rebukes and vexations, for he provoked them exceedingly. Nevertheless, he detained them at his table almost until the light of day. They lay down to sleep a bit and when it was full light, the Besh't rose to recite the dawn vatikin service. For it was his pious habit not to set out on a journey before prayers.

When they wished to proceed on their way, their host closed the door,

- Look here, I have prepared everything for your meal.

Offering to pay for all they had eaten, they asked leave not to partake of food with him again. Gesturing wildly, as if to murder them all, he shouted,

- Am I a thief that I will take your ma'ot for naught?

There was nothing for it but to again partake of food with him, and thus they tarried in his company until evening. Fearing to travel into the dangerous forest at that hour, they had to sleep in his house one more night. On the next day it was the same as the day before. And so it went.

Until the fourth day of Shabbos week, when he accepted payment for the food they had eaten. Perhaps now they were rid of him. But no, he wished to accompany them, and now they feared that the man plotted murder.

Suddenly, one of the closed doors in that house opened and a wealthy, finely adorned woman emerged from one room. She came before the Besh't and said,

- Rebbe, I ask that you pass Shabbos in my home.

The Besh't replied,

- Oh! There are two wonders here! The first: how do you know that I am the Besh't? If so, how did you allow me to pass Shabbos in desecration and with such a great unhappiness as I experienced here? Why did you not appear before this moment?

She replied,

- Do you not know me?
- No.
- I am Sarah.

Still he did not know her. And she said,

- Rebbe, remember that in such and such year I was your servant. Orphaned of my mother and my father, I was afflicted with boils. It was the lady, your wife, who made me very unhappy. Each Shabbat eve she would comb through my hair with a scraping comb. Once I shouted very much and I did not allow that she touch my head. This caused her stress and she struck my cheek. Although you observed my ordeal, you did not protest. You were silent in the face of my unhappiness.

- Your behavior caused the Holy One himself, Hallowed Be His Name, to be angered against you, for you transgressed the verse, "You shall not cause a widow or an orphan to suffer." A verdict was passed in the celestial court that you were to lose your share in the world to come that had been prepared for you.

- However, I married this man, who is a zaddik and a hidden hasid. When we learned that your matter was not favorable in the heavens, we prayed that the difficult decree be removed from you. This caused the upper court to decree − in place of the harsher judgement − that you must experience one Sabbath day in total misery, as the Sabbath is our taste of the world to come in this life. This would be a just replacement of the original verdict. Seeing that there was no one in this world who would agree to disturb your Shabbos, we decided to ourselves do this, and this is the reason for your wretched and joyless day!

Immediately, in that moment, the great wisdom of the Besh't returned to him, and he could see that the woman had spoken justice and truth. Together with his students, he traveled to her home and all passed the Sabbath in delight and rejoicing. And all the day they and their zaddik host were occupied with words of Torah.

The Temporal Bazaar

When he was a young and impoverished avrech, Rabbi Moshe Leib of Sasov was supported in the needs and necessities of his household by a certain generous gevir who was his neighbor. One day the gevir, who was an important patrician among the Jews, proposed to Rabbi Moshe Leib,

- Our most-learned one must see to the future of his children and household. Therefore, does it serve a purpose when I give him some hundreds each week? Would it not be more suitable that I give him an honorable sum with which he will try his hand at business? And surely the Almighty will help him to succeed. Hearkening to this advice, the rabbi accepted a larger sum of money from the gevir, following which he accompanied several merchants to the fair to purchase merchandise for trade. When they arrived at the city where the fair was being held, each merchant went his own way seeking food for his household. And Rabbi Moshe Leib went to the bet midrash to study and pray, remaining there as long as was his wont. When he did come to the market square, all the merchants were making ready to return home. So he said to them,

- But I came here in order to sell goods and I have yet to purchase in the market. The merchants laughed at him,

- But the day has already turned! Market day at the bazaar has come and gone.

Then they journeyed home. When Rabbi Moshe Leib came to his home, his sons came out to meet him. They turned round and round about him, asking, - Father, father, what have you brought us from the bazaar?

At this, the rabbi's reason suddenly weakened, he sickened and fell to his bed. When the gevir then came to ask what succcesses and enterprise he had encountered, he found Moshe Leib abed suffering of a broken heart,

- What is this, rebbe? Have you lost all your money? And perhaps you gave all the money I gave you to charity? Just say the word, and I will give you double that amount. After a while, when Rabbi Moshe Leib's spirit returned to him, he looked at the gevir and said,

- A man travels from his house for a day or two days. When he returns, his sons ask, "Father what have you brought us from the bazaar?" And I have nothing to reply to them. What will be when I die and arrive at the world of truth and I am asked, "What have you brought with you?" What will I reply to them? Oi to me and woe for that day of reproof, when the Almighty brings each man and woman in Israel to judgment.

- Seeing that Rabbi Moshe Leib was not suited to the ways of the everyday world, the gevir said to him,

- I now know that your Most-Learned Honor must remain here to learn Torah and deal with his household.

From that day on, the gevir disclosed to the world that Rabbi Moshe Leib Sasov was an exceptional zaddik. He became known at the gates, and Jews came from far and wide to hear his wisdom and ask his advice. From then on, Rabbi Moshe Leib Sasov was esteemed highly as a rebbe in Israel.

The Power of Remorse

There was a certain city in which resided a slanderer, a Jew who was a sore trouble to his fellow Jews. In his calumny in service of the Duke who was proprietor of the city, he was very much hated by all the community and there was no one who could profess to hold an affection for this man. He feared to walk alone in the city, even in daylight, and therefore two gentile guards always accompanied him, by order of the Duke.

Once, this informer learned of a certain secret matter and he knew that this bit of slander would earn him a tidy sum, for he earned much money for his labors. Now since the Duke lived two parasangs distance from the city, the informer harnessed his horses before dark and with two guards set out to his master's house.

When he had gone about one parasang distance from the city, he stopped his carriage near to one hostelry and seeing that the day had turned, he was reminded that he had not yet prayed the afternoon minchah prayer. Washing his hands according to ritual, he stood himself erect to recite the Shmone Esre prayer. When he arrived at the passage, "- Forgive us Our Father for we have transgressed," suddenly his soul clearly heard the words that he was uttering with his mouth. Here he was, on a journey of slander against his people. Surely they would be harmed by what he was about to tell the Duke. And he asked forgiveness for his sins.

While he was pondering these truths, he began to work out an account of his soul and was recalled of each and every slander he had ever spoken. Laboring at this for a while, all his transgressions soon were posed before him in a great heap. Bitterly, he ceased his prayers, for how could he say, "Forgive us Our Father for we have transgressed"? And now he was very regretful of all he had done. Taking upon himself the abandonment of his sinful ways from that time on, he decided to return immediately to his home and not to continue on to the Duke. However, the fear that the Duke would punish him if he did not appear before him to transmit the slander as was his custom waged a war in his heart. Turning these matters over and over in his mind, he made up his mind as follows: "No matter what is done to me, I will not say a word. Even if the Duke will tear me to shreds and beat me until my soul passes from my body."

He took this resolution upon himself with a whole heart, delaying for a long time over the prayer, "For give us, o' Lord, for we have sinned." until the matter was stamped upon his heart forever. He would never dare hand a Jew over to the authorities again; he would abandon his sinful ways and never enact such evil again.

The guards who accompanied him saw that, with groans and secret weepings, he had taken a long time for his prayers. This seemed a wonder in their eyes but, although they had not observed him drink chnapps all that day, at first they believed that he was drunk and had become foolish in his cups. Not knowing what to make of it, they called out to him, but he did not reply. They waited until they were tired of waiting, that he might finish his praying, but they could see by his face that he was deeply lost in his unhappiness and groaning. When he was finished praying, the guards said to him,

- What has happened to you today that you weep long in prayers? Are you planning to become a rabbi?

The man replied,

- My head is heavy on my shoulders. Therefore, I will return now to my home and rest the night. Tomorrow, I will set out again to see the Duke.

- Now we understand! It is clear that you have fabricated some lie in your heart.

The man denied this, but they did not accept his words,

- We continue to the Duke and you will say your piece there.

Pleading that the guards leave him be, he offered them a gift of money. But they refused to accept under any circumstances, nor did they permit him to return home.

Thereupon, they journeyed to the Duke who asked the informer,

- Have you brought some news with you?

- No.

- Then, why have you come here if you have no news?

He replied as well he could, but the guards told the Duke that although when they set out from the city, he declared, "I am going to tell the Duke a thing which is very important. I have learned of a concealed matter and will whisper it into his ear." when he stopped for afternoon prayer, he began to weep and moan. And after that, he asked to return home.

When the Duke heard this, he became very angry. He slapped the informer's face and began to beat him, anxious to hear the scandalous news. But the Jew accepted the beating and did not say a word. The Duke increased his blows threefold but the Jew said nothing. Then the Duke threw him out of the manor. The man harnessed his horse, climbed aboard the wagon and went on his way.

Now, as he was departing the manor estate, he could hear a great wailing. Following the troubled sounds, he soon found a woman standing near the road without her clothing, crying out bitterly and with all her might. The man asked her,

- What is this?

Then she told him this tale,

- From this certain village do I come and this is the night of the month that I must immerse myself in the river and be cleansed for my husband. Thus, did I travel to the river and my husband was waiting for me, and my clothing was in the wagon with him. Suddenly the horse became frightened and ran wildly off with the wagon and all my clothing; and my husband after it. I remained here naked, without my clothes, and it grows colder. Then I began to run about and lost my way. The man rushed to remove his cloak and to cover her nakedness. He helped her onto the wagon and brought her home. Then he went to look for her husband, to tell him that he had saved his wife's life and that she was at home. The man thanked him and went home. And the man who had been an informer and who saved his wife also journeyed home.

The very next day, the penitent fell to his bed and was ill. The people of the town were very happy since they had no knowledge of what had happened the night before. When they learned that the slanderer, who handed Jews over to the authorities, was closer to death than to life, the rejoicing in the town was high and all were relieved. For this slanderer had troubled them greatly, and they wished that he would never rise again from his sick bed.

So it was. The man died before evening.

The rabbi of that city, who was a great zaddik, did not wish the dead man to be shamed at the funeral, and he announced to all the townspeople that he would not permit the heart of any man to humiliate the deceased, saying,

- The man will pay for his transgressions in the World of Truth, and what do you have to do with it?

Many townspeople participated in the funeral because all were happy at the informer's death, that they were now rid of

210

Funeral Procession - J. Steinhart

such an evil affliction as this. He was buried and no man knew the truth of what happened in his soul at his end.

Three days after the death of the informer, the husband of the woman whom he had saved from death came to ask the rabbi an intimatel question of halacha,

- I have come to ask the rabbi if I am permitted to cohabit with my wife? And the matter is as follows. On the evening that our horse and wagon ran off, she remained naked and alone with the informer who brought her home. Although she says that she was not ravished, can she be trusted for her word? Perhaps she is afeared of me and does not want to be divorced, and perhaps she is not telling the truth. Not only that, but the informer had the reputation of a transgressor and I do not believe that this immoral man did not tempt and have his way with my wife. Then she is forbidden to me; I am not permitted to cohabitate with her.

The rabbi did not know what to reply, and said to him,

- Go and return here tomorrow.

That night, the rabbi zaddik performed a "question within a dream." that he might learn from the celestial world what was the verdict regarding the wife of this man.

In the dream, the celestial powers revealed to him that the informer had fully repented of his transgressions during the minchah prayer the day before he died. After this, he was sorely tested in his meeting with the Duke, but did not speak perversion of any Jew although many blows and beatings were his lot. For this reason, he was called upon from the heavens to fulfill the greatest of all mitzvot – the saving of a human life. Notwithstanding the temptation which he faced in saving the naked woman, he did not permit his passion to incite and prompt him to commit a severe transgression. Therefore, and because of these things, he passed from the corporeal world as a total penitent; one who has earned his place in the world to come.

And Gan Eden was ensured to him forevermore.

212

THE CELESTIAL GATES

A New Heart and a New Spirit Will I Put Within You

The learned author of "Hachnasat Orchim", The Mitzvah of Hospitality, wrote of the following,: I had a brother who was older than I in years. This brother, of noble and excellent spirit, was given of true, esoteric wisdoms, and in his youth, the prophet Eliyahu, well remembered to all, was revealed to him. Whereas I, was more skilled than my brother in the understanding of known and illuminated Torah and the task of declaring halachic decisions. We sat together thus in love and affection from Shabbos to Shabbos, as brothers dwelling in unity. And we earned our livelihood by means of a tavern which our father had left us in inheritance.

Time passed, and my brother's only daughter became of age. A match was made for her with a man suitable and of fine character. Now, the income from the tavern was not sufficient to pay for the cost of the wedding, and my elder brother, occupied with his learning, never thought to concern himself with the mundane. For his faith in the blessed Almighty was complete and whole.

Nevertheless, as the nuptial day grew near and I sensed that the tavern could not supply the income to pay for the many needs of the wedding, - to say nothing of a sufficient income for the daily needs of both our homes. Thus, I began to talk of this matter with my brother, at which time he said,

- Whatever you advise me to do I will surely fulfill, everything according to your wise suggestion, because I myself know naught of the ways of the world.

It was then that I told him my plan,

- Listen to me my brother and my friend, for I will advise you. It is our knowledge that the Blessed One, Holy be His Name, created the world in such a way to allow His creatures to conduct themselves in an orderly fashion and not disturb Him daily with all manner of requests for radical reform and change for improving one's lot. Thus, it seems to me that in the natural way of our lives, the revenue from the tavern should have been sufficient for the many wedding costs. Too, the women must have fine dresses sewn. Therefore, it is my suggestion that I separate from you. You will remain here with the tavern which will furnish your household needs and also the wedding costs. I will sojourn with my family and find dwelling in a city where a community of our brethren Israel has need of a rabbi or a Rosh Yeshiva, or at the least, I can instruct infants in Torah. My salary will suffice for my household. You, my brother, have no such opportunity to seek out earnings for your family, since you occupy yourself with unusual excellence in matters of celestial truths and wisdom, and are forbidden to make use of this wisdom in the material world, especially for your livelihood.

My brother listened to my faithful words for his good, and they appealed to him. But his heart was saddened for the parting. Therefore, while he accepted my proposal, he began also to ponder thoughts of other remedies so that brothers would not have to be divided. But none was found and, since

216

financial distress will not be ignored, my brother accepted my plan.

Having made ready for the journey by purchasing a horse and vehicle to transport my family, my brother and his household labored for all our needs. A traveler's costume was sewn for me with shoulder sack, and a walking stick fashioned. Bread was dried and wrapped, and a waterskin sewn to place on my back; all things customary for a long journey.

The parting was an agony for us both. For brother must be sundered from brother. As we set out, my household and myself were blessed by my brother, as one does accompany a dear one along his way. And at the last, he called out to me the verse spoken by the Almighty to Father Abraham: "Go you from your land and your birthplace and the home of your father, to a land which I show to you, and I will bless and increase your name and you will be for a blessing." He embraced me and kissed me, and we each wept boundless tears on the shoulder of the other.

At the first town nearest to our city I spoke with the townspeople, offering myself for the position of rabbi. They said,

- Our Rabbi has not yet worn down his skills.

Too in the matter of infant's Torah teacher they turned me away, saying,

- The city is rich in learned men and scholarly teachers, and why do we need you to bring wine to our overflowing kegs?

In extreme poverty and wretchedness we continued along the road, that I might pitch our tent further on in another town, where wefound no rest for our feet. Again I burdened my horse and continued far to wander, that we might find a livelihood. But the distance of several parasangs between myself and the city of my birth had not been to our gain. The idea entered my heart that I might retrace my steps and return home, but I thought, "Let us go a bit farther". I pitched my tent in another city where we ate of the bitter herb and drank bitter draught. For there was no one to give an ear, that I might serve as rabbi and spiritual leader to their community or instruct their children in the Torah. No community wished to maintain me.

When the last penny had gone from my pocket, I said to myself, "Now I must return home, to the city of my birth." When I discussed our return with my household, they said,

- If the money is ended, how can we return such a far distance? Better to travel on ahead. Perhaps the Blessed Almighty will have compassion and find a community for our livelihood.

- But the costs of the journey forward are to great, and I have not a penny.

- Woe! Woe! The hand of the Lord has come down upon us. You must think a thought which will bring us food. In the next city we go immediately the house of the parnass. You present yourself as a darshan, and deliver moral sermons to the people. In this way, you will help cleanse them of sin and this will be to your credit in the eyes of the Almighty. As for us, your family, there will be deliverance in your earnings.

This advice of my household fell pleasing upon my ears, although I was not accustomed to this particular occupation. For as they say, true need helps one to forbear disgrace. And so it was. I began to deliver sermons in each and every city, and this offered us food and sustenance for a long while. But the day came that our clothing was worn and shabby, and Jews no longer gave ear to my admonishing sermons. For, as the wisest of men, King Solomon, said in Qohelet, "The poor man's wisdom is despised, his words are not attended to." At that time, we were brought so low as to beg from door to door for a penny, the most humble and miserable paupers.

Much time went by, and I was now more than 200

parasangs from the city of my birth, a great distance from our country's borders. Accustomed to our penury, we passed our lives in the manner of those beggars who wander from city to town. And the troubles of the road had weakened us considerably.

One time, I descended from the straight road onto a twisted track, a path unknown even to hawks and eagles. Soon, we were lost in a maze of forest with no open expanse around. But the Almighty had compassion and did removed us from this forest. And so it was.

Wandering without path or sign for three days and nights until we had not a morsel to keep our souls alive, and were swathed in our misfortune. Our horse was faint with exceeding weakness and had forgotten his master's stall, for I could not care for him properly. The skies darkened with heavy clouds and a far-sweep of rain began, bringing more woe onto our heads. We sank into a deep stress of mud and siege of mire and a great trouble was upon us.

I prayed to the Almighty that he might save us, and hearing my prayer, He extracted us from this prison. I was directed down to a paved road, a straight way through an unplowed field until we came to a large inn, a very fine building. I knocked on the door, and here, an elderly man, cloaked in a woolen garment of sheepskin typical of the humble folk, rose to meet me. This man's face burned bright as a torch, and was as radiant as the sun at the noon hour. He opened the gate for us with an expression of vast joy which I cannot well describe, as though he were welcoming a bride and groom; after which, he led my horse to feed and stall. Then, taking up my small children and carrying them on his wings as though he were the proud eagle, he were welcomed us into his house. All these things were accompanied by his delight as with a found treasure. Then he said to us all,

- Welcome you who entered under the shadow of my eaves.

Seeing the great happiness on the countenance of this old man, I became frightened and remained standing where I was, atremble and wary lest he be a thief, thus welcoming us as though we were some found fortune.

Seeing my hesitation and that I was concerned, he spoke gently,

- Pardon sir. For this humble dwelling is not on your esteemed level.

He brought us into the inner room where were tables pleasantly set, on them all kinds of delicacies and the most excellent wines. Many people were seated at these tables, eating and drinking and of glad heart. The old man readied us a table with his own hands. Then we ate and drank and the generous hand of the Almighty was extended to us. We recited the grace after food, and blessed the householder as is the custom. The old man troubled himself again and again to rise and serve the people and ourselves. Observing this, I imagined in my heart that perhaps this festive table was a particular celebration for the unseen householder and that the old man was his servant.

Afterwards, when our hearts were at peace, the old man brought us into a special room where there were beautiful beds of tapestry-woven Egyptian yarn, inviting us to rest from the strains of our journey. When we awoke from our sleep, I prayed the minchah service and then the evening Aravit service according to Jewish tradition. Then the old man came to say,

- Time has come for the evening meal.

I saw that all the people who had eaten in the afternoon had gone on their way, and other travelers were come that evening in their place. Again the old man went to welcome them. Again, he laid the tables with various kinds of food and drink and attended everyone with his own hand.

Drawing – L. Reis

I now understood the matter well. This house was not a bad affliction, the Almighty forbid, nor was there a family wedding celebration. The old man's joy was for his performing the mitzvah of hospitality, just as our Father Abraham, of blessed memory, had welcomed all strangers into his tent and hurried to prepare food and drink. For he was happy to delight the heart of the Almighty and His people. Then I understood that the old man was the householder himself. His fervor was due to the Holy one granting him the privilege of performing this mitzvah. This caused me pleasure, and I thanked the Blessed One in all His great good for granting us this night and someone to watch over us.

On the next day I arose to continue on my way but the old man did not permit me to leave. And he said ,

- Look here and see, I do not know why you are in a hurry to go on your way. I observe that you are troubled and frightened, wandering here and there from place to place, knocking on doors and begging for food for your family. What loss if today you rest and pleasure yourselves to again eat at my table as you did yesterday?

He implored my family exceedingly, and in this way we tarried at his house for a full eight days, and were deeded much honor and cordiality.

During those days I asked about his position and welfare. He was an important man indeed, but did not deal in business himself, for his family were merchants. He did not partake of any of the delicacies, and to satisfy his soul he ate only small amounts and was sated. Conducting himself as one of the paupers of Israel, all his life was directed towards performing the mitzvah of hosting guests with great joy and serving them with his own hands. He had no other occupation, only this one mitzvah, like our Father Abraham. Thus, I had the privilege to observe a man who sought only to please the Creator, Blessed be His name, in our generation.

He grew close to myself and my family and showed an exceptionally sweet nature. For several days I sat and talked with him,

- And what will the end be, when will I travel home? For there is no purpose in my sitting here, I must travel on and perhaps the Almighty will find some livelihood for me.

Again, the old man implored me greatly that I stay several days more. When the time did come to part from him and to be on our way, he prepared food for our journey, fodder for our horse and accompanied us along the road. When we parted from him in peace, I asked him,

- What is it that you lack? For I wish to bless you and ask that the Almighty fulfill all your needs.

He replied and said,

- I lack for nothing, glory to the Blessed Almighty.

I asked again,

- Perhaps you have some request from the Monarch of the Universe, the King of Kings, the Holy One?

Then, with a broken heart, he murmered,

- One great request do I have, since I have no son. I believe that my hopes have been abandoned for I, and also my wife, may she live until 120, have seen many days, and how could we have a child so late in years?

When I heard and saw this, I trembled and my heart turned over within me; my innermost parts were moved to think that strangers would be the inheritance of this kosher and upright man. Therefore, I said with great force of intention,

- I am confident that my elder brother, a man of G-d who favored me thus before out parting, "And thou shalt be a blessing to others", has given me the gift of bestowing a blessing upon you. And I say that next year at this season you and your wife will embrace a son and his name in Israel will be Yosef.

I parted from him in peace and went on my way, traveling hither and yon, until the Almighty found for me one large city under His heaven, where I was accepted as rabbi and as rosh yeshiva. And my family and I myself settled there.

So it was, my blessing to the old man was heard by the Almighty, and his wife came to be with child. A son was born, his name in Israel, Yosef. His father called him Yosale and arranged a great feast on the day that the boy was to enter into the covenant of our Father Abraham, the day of the Brit Milah. Every year, on his son's birth date, he would hold a festive meal in honor of the child and invite all the people of his city. He also gave charity in the boy's name with a generous heart, and distributed alms to all the poor.

But this boy born to him did not grow in the natural way. At the age of three his size was as age seven, and when he was seven he was as twenty years in height. Sadly, in wisdom it was the reverse. When he was twenty years old his mind was as a seven year old child, and when seven, he was as three. When he was three years old, his sense was as a one day old infant. A fool, and mad without measure, he posessed no insight of heart to understand the shape of a word at all. A great mantle of red hair covered his head and body, his features were extremely coarse and his voice thick. His legs were very long and as broad as an angry bear, for which reason he walked barefoot and refused to wear shoes. The father was greatly sorrowed by this son.

Time passed and the hand of the Almighty caused the old man's house to burn down and be destroyed, and all his cattle to be afflicted and die. After several days his wife also died. Then the old man himself died and the boy Yosale was left without father and mother, bereft of sense, and a pauper without bread or clothing.

The community who had well known the old father were

sick to their souls to see all the humiliation which the only son of this old man did suffer. With all their efforts, they tried to teach him some blessing or prayer so that at least he should be worthy of the name Jew. But they did not succeed in their efforts because he was mad by nature, without comprehension, and a fool. They became discouraged and left him alone to himself, to wander about idle. Finally, by reason of their broken heart for the old man, his father, and so that the mad boy might not serve as a degradation and a shame to his father's memory, they sent him from their city in the company of a team of traveling beggars. Yosale wandered from city to town with them as their servant. Every morning and evening he would go from door to door of a town to beg for slices of bread, and brought his cache to the beggars. Thus he ate and drank and was sustained.

This went on for a long time. Yosale learned no prayer at all and even did not know that there was an Almighty in the world. He only knew to eat and be replete from what each day's windfall, to devour and be satisfied for the moment. No matter if the food were kosher or treif, profane or pure, it was all the same to him. The boy Yosale wandered from city to town and from town to village, and one day the band of beggars arrived at the city where I myself had made my home and served as rabbi and rosh yeshiva.

During those years, I had heard nothing of the old man and his son. But Yosale, who was quick to find each house and gather bread slices for the paupers who cared for him, happened to arrive at our door. He begged a slice of bread from my wife, the rebbezin, and she gave him what she had. But Yosale refused it, demanding more. The matter developed until Yosale was quarreling with the mother of my sons. He began to blaspheme her with emphatic curses and complain in his heavy and coarse voice.

When the yeshivah students heard all this, they came to help my wife him and to cast the ruffian out of the house.

225

Then he began to shout a great and bitter shout, until I heard it where I was. Immediately, I stepped from my study-room to learn the meaning of this hue and cry. What was this and about what? Seeing this unfortunate beggar whom the students wished to cast him out, I admonished them and brought him before me, greeting him with the word, "Shalom." He replied "Shalom". I asked him,

- From what city are you?

But he did not wish to reply or speak with me at all until I soothed him with kind and gentle words. I distracted and calmed him until the anger was gone from his heart and asked again,

- What city are you from?

He replied,

- I am Yosale the son of the elder so-and-so who used to live on the roadside on the way to this particular city. My father had a fine house and great wealth.

When I heard this, I knew that this boy was the son of the old man, the master of hospitality. And I knew that he had been born to the old man and his wife from the blessing I had given them. My heart rejoiced for this and I was glad that my blessing had been heard. But I was also very pained that from my blessing such a foolish and mad boy had been born, different from other human beings. I asked him,

- How is your father?

He replied that his father and his mother were dead, and said,

- It is good for me to beg from door to door, for my father used to beat me all day. Now that my father and mother are dead and their home burned down, it is good because I can do as my heart pleases and no one can protest.

He continued, telling me that he had joined up with a band of beggars,

- I am their servant, begging for food. I am their leader and I have two pockets in my coat, one pocket for meat and

226

milk foods, and the second pocket for other kinds of pauper's needs and all the kinds of food which I see in the houses of the city. Now I ask that you give me what I wish and if you do not do so in a good way, I will take it from you by force.

When I heard the words of this boy who had been born of my blessing, I was sorry to the death, and remembered how his father, of blessed memory, had the superior traits of our Father Abraham. His son, this boy, was such a coarse fool, and every blemish that could be suffered by man was his. I recalled also the wealth of his father, and the pleasure which he caused to others. Now he was gone and lost. And his only son was such a one as this! Woe! My innards raged within me and I called out,

- Lord of the Universe, Is this Torah and can this be the Torah's earnings? G-d forbid that this be the reward of such a man who labored and made himself weary in the service of others. For all his fortune was intended only for others to enjoy and be happy. Every man who entered his home hungry as a homeless dog, left there well fed. Is it possible that the mitzvah with which this zaddik occupied himself would fail thus in his seed? It is forbidden, Judge of all Creation, that such a thing as this should be.

The conclusion of it was that I took the boy Yosale aside and spoke kind words to comfort him,

- Your father has died and there is no one to raise you; why not eat the afternoon meal at my table?

- No, I do not wish it. With the paupers I eat what I wish and when I wish. With you I shall sit at a table under your eye and be polite. Here, I must eat slowly and in a leisurely way and I am not accustomed to this. No, I do not want this thing.

I continued,

- Listen my son, I will instruct that you be given everything that your heart desires.

227

- What will I gain if you feed me the afternoon meal? And what of the evening meal? Also, this will delay me from returning to the beggar band and they will be angry with me. Then I will be left alone and lost in my many troubles, since alone my life is bitter.

- In the evening too you will eat with us.

- But what of tomorrow? For in the end I will have to return to the beggars and ask their help.

- I wish you always to be seated at my table. I will dress you in silken and embroidered clothing.

And the fool replied,

- Nevertheless, I do not want this.

I labored long and troubled myself until he agreed to stay in my home. All the members of my household and my students were amazed at this thing, for they did not know that I bore a moral debt to return this boy to a decent state for the honor of his elderly father. And that by reason of my blessing this fool had been born to him.

After the boy-fool had been in the serenity of my home several days, enjoying honor and splendor and all the pleasures of man, his heart was calmed, and he took his place as one of my family. The paupers left him to his own devices and went on their way. Then I began gently to bring the boy close, wishing to educate and teach him the Hebrew letters of the "aleph - bet", hoping to open for him the haven of the Shekhinah, for the sake of his old father's honor. But he could not comprehend even the shape of the letter "aleph", and all my efforts were to no avail. Sorrowed beyond belief, I watched the gluttonous fool eating and stumbling along, always bare of foot and slave only to the wanton desires of his heart. Then he began to incite quarrels among my students and my household and harmed everyone, striking them and blaspheming as one lacking reason is wont to do. All manner of foolery were his mode,

228

and in the night hours, he wandered about, tearing at his clothing.

The only good trait in him was that he would obey me in all matters of errand. So much so that if I would order that he throw himself into a burning pyre to remove an item from there, he would obey me. When I understood that my plan to instruct him failed, that this boy would never be able to learn Torah and to behave with derech eretz, and when I saw that his only skill was to obey me in matters of errand, I appointed him to be the messenger of the bet din.

The boy Yosale, every place where I dispatched him, hastened there quickly, and nothing in the world served to delay him, neither torrent of downpour, nor wind nor snow nor the cold at all. Now, this matter was very much to the benefit of the bet din, since there was an urgent need to enact the Torah decisions quickly and according to the letter of the law.

Thus it was that the Almighty blessed me in this and Yosale was a success as my messenger. By virtue of Yosale's unusual degree of eager speed, no ruling of justice was delayed for even one day. Never did Yosale lag even one moment when he walked on a mission for the bet din, not for any reason. On the very day of his errand it was completed. When I dispatched him to call litigants to judgment who resided a three day walking distance, Divine Providence would cause that the man being sued was walking in the direction of the bet din at that very hour. This matter was both a wonder and a great joy to me, and I said, surely the virtue of his elderly father has granted him this success in his errands.

A long time passed, during which I served as Presiding Judge of the Bet Din in this city. One day a letter arrived from my elder brother. He instructed that I obey his call to return with my family so that we could again be together as brothers should be, as was our wont during our early years.

My elder brother's longing to see me was exceedingly strong and our separation was very painful for him. He also wrote that I should choose a young man from among my yeshiva students, excellent and learned in Torah, to serve as groom for his modest daughter who was gifted with many most excellent and meritorious traits.

Now, this was a very difficult matter. After many years of struggle and labor and the bitter experiences which had overtaken us, I had achieved comfort. Thanks to the Almighty, I lived in peace and respect, serving as the rabbi and spiritual leader of this city. But, if my older brother, a true man of G-d and a holy person, commanded, I must obey. Thereupon, I invited all the parnassim and the Jewish folk of the city, and informed them of the contents of my brother's letter, explaining that I must obey him and return to the city of my birth.

It was decided to voyage by sea so as to shorten the journey , for I did not wish to delay long days as when we had traveled from our city through the towns and barren lands. We prepared all that we would need for a sea voyage, and also foodstuffs for all members of the family. Then my family asked,

- What will we do with the boy Yosale, will we take him with us? For we must set sail on a dangerous journey. Also, we must carry enough food for all the children and measure it by amount and weight as people do when they go down to the sea in ships. What is our connection to this troublesome fool, that we must also take him – one who eats as a glutton and will devour all the food we have prepared for the voyage in one day. . . We will all remain bereft at sea, without sustenance. Not only this, but by reason of his loud voice and anger at not being given all the food he demands, he will capsize the ship. We say that the danger of being killed by reason of his anger is greater than the danger of a storm at sea. Many souls will be endangered!

Therefore, their advice was that Yosale be left behind.

I agreed and I took the advice of my household, and we consulted between us how this would be possible. By reason of his great lack of sense and also his speed it would be difficult to part from him. On the other hand, we could think of no way to conceal the matter of our voyage, since by virtue of his particular skills he would learn that we were leaving him.

Deciding that in three days' time we would go down to the sea and board the ship, I sent Yosale to a far city, three parasangs walk away, to call on one man to appear at the bet din. Surely he would delay there for at least three days, because the one being sued was a violent man. But as soon as Yosale had left the city, here the ba'al din came walking up to him. Yosale gave the court petition into his hand and brought the litigant to court that very day.

When we saw that my plan had been disturbed, I sent Yosale to an even more distant address. I thought to myself that now surely we would be able to leave, and when the boy returned to the city he would no longer find us. Hurriedly, we went down to the dock that very day and settled ourselves inside the ship, but again he was most successful, and met the man summoned as he was departing the city. When Yosale entered the bet din and there was no one there, he understood that we had sailed. Then he ran quickly down to the seashore and, as the Almighty wished it, since the ship had not yet sailed from the dock, Yosale jumped onto the ship. We saw that the fool was very successful and we could not escape him; whatever he wished, he achieved. Then he began to curse and reproach us for wishing to leave him behind, but we could not reply because we were frightened.

We set sail and after two days at sea, a great storm blew up and the waves towered high above us, casting us into a frozen sea where the ship sank deep into icy waters. All the

231

sailors know that there was no cure or advice for this. We were dependent on the will of the Almighty, that He might save us. And He brought the waters up with a great storm wind, and the ship was removed from the frozen waters into clear waters. But here too we had no hope, for where we were directed was a lofty mountain, its peak towering high into the firmament. The steep elevation of the mountain blocked off the wind which could steer our sails out of that bay.

The rocky mountain peak was also too high to climb, and we could see many ancient remains of ships which had gone down to the sea and been washed up there. The bones of those who had sailed in them were strewn on the shore. Knowing then that we had no hope and were to die there of starvation, our weeping and keening grew loud. And we saw with our eyes that the day of our death was near.

I parcelled out the remaining food so that it should maintain us for a time, but the boy Yosale had no sorrow, nor did he groan by reason of the calamity. So long as he had food and was well fed for the moment, he was pleased and nothing else entered his mind. Food sufficient for one person for three days, sufficed him for only one. Satisfied, he did not concern himself with the morrow. When the bread which we had given him was no more, he dug secretly into our food cache and that of all the passengers and ate everyone's share as well.

When the ship's passengers learned that the bread was gone from their cache before they had eaten it, for Yosale had stolen everything, all came to me with great weeping and groaning, spirits and bodies bent, calling out that Yosale had stolen all their food,

- Why did you bring a Hebrew man who is such a fool and mad, that we might perish and our end be brought closer?

The end of it was that I scolded Yosale,

- Why did you do this and steal all the food of the ship's

passengers? Go now to the top of the mountain and eat grass of the land.

Yosale replied,

- Yes, I will, I will.

He began to climb and could not. But by excess of unhappiness, he dug and carved the wall of the mountain with the fingernails of his hand and feet, like a human gimlet. He climbed the mountain with all his strength and the force of his courage, and remained there all that day. On the mountain top, he walked along the peak for a long distance where he saw many trees of pleasant appearance bearing fruit excellent to eat. He picked the fruit and filled his belly until he was satisfied. Then he took an amount, stored it inside his shirt and hurried to bring it down to us. He seemed to be mocking us,

- Here! I have climbed to the top of the mountain and eaten, now you also eat of this fruit.

When the passengers witnessed this wonder, they all declared it was by virtue of Yosale's rabbi, and all thanked the Almighty, the G-d of Israel. But I myself knew that it was not due to myself, but only by the virtue of Yosale's elderly father and his important mitzvah of hospitality. We were saved by reason of his splendid spirit. So, I said to Yosale,

- My son, this will now be your task. Each and every day in the morning you will arise and climb high onto the mountain. After you have eaten and are satisfied, you will bring us food to keep our souls alive.

And so it was. We sewed two great pockets into his garment to hold as much fruit as he could carry. Every day he rose early to do his task eagerly and swiftly as we had instructed and all the ship's passengers ate of the fruit. This situation continued for a long while, until I began to consider that we should learn what there was on top of this mountain. Perhaps we could remove ourselves from the mud and refuse here below. Now, I told the boy Yosale,

- When you climb the mountain, I instruct you to walk along the length and width to see whether you can find a settlement. Then return to me.

This he did. Climbing the mountain peak, he walked the length and width until he came to one wall of iron at the southern edge and there were etched many round and square niches, short and long in shape. Yosale thought to take hold of the holes with his fingernails but did not succeed and could not climb that wall. He returned to me sadly, bringing fruit as was his habit, and told me all that had happened,

- I saw there a wall of iron, very high and smooth and erect, on which are niches, but I could not take hold of them to climb.

I myself understood that on the etched niches were written letters, and Yosale could not understand this, for he knew not how to read.

- Take this wax mold with you tomorrow when you climb the mountain. Go to the iron wall and press the wax into all the niches, up and down. Remove the wax carefully, that the raised portion not become flat and the flat portion not become raised. Then bring the wax in its entirety to me, so that I can know what is written there.

Yosale did well in all that I had instructed. Although he understood nothing, his success was fine and the matter was well done in his hands. He removed the wax with care and brought it down the mountain to me. It showed clearly the etchings on the iron wall. I saw the letters and the words and connected them together to read,

"Let it be known that here is the lower level of Gan Eden, and the sea and the mountain and the wall stand guard so that no one can enter this place. When Israelites have been brought here by the frozen sea, they must recite these certain passages from David's Psalms on the days mentioned here. They must cast their thoughts into these particular divine intentions and fast the certain fast days noted here, and pray the \ prayers which appear here. And when the particular and correct tikkun which has been destined for them will be achieved by their soul, their ship will be lifted up in one single moment and returned to calm seas."

I read these words, and was filled with joy and I thanked the Almighty for the good with which He had benefited us. I immediately began to conduct pious penance and fasts such as described on the wax impression, and the boy Yosale climbed the mountain as was his habit to fill his stomach every day and to bring us fruit.

When the tikkun to our souls came upon us in perfect wholeness, in one moment a wind was brought mightily forward to carry the ship from where it lay, back onto a smooth and calm sea.

At that time Yosale was on the mountain, and when he descended and saw the ship had sailed on its way, he raised his voice in reproach and bitter weeping. I too, when I saw Yosale not with us in the ship when the tikkun came upon us, raised my voice in weeping and lamentation for him; because Yosale had saved our souls and brought us sustenance to keep us alive. Was this to be his fate? Surely he would now remain in the frozen waters and die there, G-d forbid and I could not find any remedy for it.

The boy Yosale, when he saw that the ship had gone, went down into the frozen sea; and when he had sunk up to his arms, he stopped there, unable to turn hither or yon. When he knew that surely he was to die, he let forth a groan which emerged from the very walls of his bosom. He carried his voice aloft and shouted and wept out of his broken heart, calling out the words,

- Oh father, my father!

Immediately his father came to him and said,

- My son, know that all these people have been delayed at the foot of this mountain for your sake. I did all these things.

235

Studying in Bialystok Bet Hamidrash - Reiss

And it was for you, so that one time in your life your heart would shatter. For since the day you were grown, not one time did your heart break, and this is why I could not succeed to create any good in you. Now that your heart has suffered within you, I will reveal to you all the secrets of the Torah.

Then his father taught him all the secrets of the Torah, those illuminated and revealed, and those secret and hidden to man. In that instant Yosale became another person.

His father made the condition that Yosale not reveal this to any man until after the blessed hour that he would stand under the wedding canopy. Then his father carried him up and brought him to stand in our ship.

When I saw Yosale in the belly of the ship, I asked,

- Who brought you here?

And he replied,

- What do you want of me? You thought me to die in the midst of the sea!

And he began to blaspheme and beat the other passengers as fools do, complaining that all were to blame and saying,

- I brought you food all those days and saved you all from death in an abyss of sea. But you returned bed for the good and abandoned me in the depths. You have caused me great suffering.

Still, the people were happy and glad of heart that the Almighty had granted no man to be harmed or taken from us. That no one was lost, not even the boy Yosale. After this, we sailed for several days until we came to the city of my birth. Descending from the ship, my family sat on the shore to rest a bit, then I dispatched one of my students to inform my brother that we were here at the dock.

The word went out that we had arrived, and all our relatives came to greet us. My saintly and esteemed brother came then and immediately asked if I had kept my word.

Had I brought with me to his house a talmid hahkam, a learned young man to be his daughter's husband.

- I have done as you instructed.

I indicated two yeshiva students whom I had brought with me that he might choose between them. But when he saw them, he said,

- I can see in the light of my soul's spirit that these are not suitable for my daughter. . . Perhaps you have another talmid hahkam.

- But my brother, these are important Torah scholars.

- I do not want them.

Then one of my family jumped forward and said to my holy brother in a jocular way,

- Here. We have another with us, a mad, coarse and filthy young man, and we have suffered terrible tribulations because of him on the journey.

And my brother said,

- Bring him to me and let us see him.

This caused all the people to laugh and mock.

Yosale came before my pious brother, whereupon he stood up and said,

- Surely the Lord's annointed stands here before me. This man is the groom which the Almighty has chosen and intended for my daughter.

When I heard these words from my brother, in my heart I thought, "Perhaps there is no error. Perhaps my brother truly sees in the spirit of his holiness that this boy is the mate for his daughter."

But I could not speak a word. Very grieved, my heart was tumultuous within me. Could such a thing be, that this mad Yosale will become the son-in-law of my dear brother? From excess of unhappiness, I fell to my bad in severe malady. And for my brother's sake, I emerged from my suffering and arose, blessed be the Creator of the Universe.

My brother instructed that Yosale be stripped of his rags

and dressed in fine clothing and embroidery. But the fool continued to behave as before, speaking mockery, and we were a ridicule before all the people of the town – that a holy man such as my brother would take for himself such a madman. And Yosale seemed to be deaf and not to hear a thing, occupied only with clowning and foolery.

The end of it was that a wedding canopy was set up, the ceremony done and all the people sat down to the feast. Then the clown, as was the custom in our town, announced that the groom should speak and enlighten us with his own words of Torah in honor of his wedding.

Only then did the groom Yosale open his mouth and say these very words,

- Whosoever feels in his soul a wavering and a wondering and the dust of transgression clings to him, he is not worthy to hear my sermon.

At that moment, the awesome fear of the Almighty came upon all the people sitting there and one by one many rose from their seats and were gone. I too felt the contents of my heart pour into my body, and I wished to escape and leave there. The groom understood that I wished to flee, and he held onto my hands, saying,

- You must hear my drasha from my mouth. And you will see that this is truely Torah and this is the reward of Torah.

All that night Yosale spoke secrets of the Torah. And from that time, the Almighty gave him a new heart and a repaired spirit He did renew within him. Yosale became known to all as a Torah prodigy and a great zaddik, as was deserving and suitable for the honor and memory of his elderly father who had excelled so greatly in the merit of hospitality.

And his son was from that time called "Rabbi Yossi".

This homiletic tale is found in an ancient book kept in the library of the city of Vienna.

The Justice of Torah

An occurance of Rabbi Abraham Yehoshua Heschel of Aphta, which came about during his service on the rabbinical chair of the city of Jassi. A Gaon, far-famed and distinguished in his generation for Torah study, and a true zaddik, Rabbi Abraham Yehoshua Heschel was also well versed in the hidden wisdoms of the Torah. However, this latter fact was not yet known to the Jews of Jassi. And all the people of the city honored and were in awe of him for he was dauntless before man, and feared only the Almighty One.

One time, Rebbetzin Heschel went down to the Street of the Fishermen to purchase a fish in honor of the Shabbat, as was her habit. And every Jew knows that a fish on the Shabbat table brings blessing to the home. But there was a shortage of fresh fish in the city and she found none for sale. Very distressed, since it had never happened that she did not cook a fish for Shabbat, she asked the fishermen to catch a fish for her and she would pay them whatever they wished. Promising to fulfill her request, two fishermen took their small boat out, and the rebbetzin waited until they returned.

After a long interval, they returned happily with two large fish for which the rebbetzin paid them much money. As she

241

took the fish from their hand, the wife of the wealthy gevir came riding along in her carriage. She had also come to purchase fish and found none. The fisherman said they had managed only to catch two fish for the wife of the rabbi. And the wife of the gevir began to shout,

- Who is this wretched pauper who must have fish on a Shabbos when all the people of the town have none? I will pay you twice what this lowly woman gave you for the fish.

As she spoke, she grabbed the fish from the hands of the rebbetzin and tossed it into her carriage. Then she climbed up and told the driver to hurry and spur the horse on and race home.

The fishermen were very angry, but they feared the wife of the gevir, who was also mayor of the city. Rebbetzin Heschel remained standing and weeping for the humiliation and the insults with which this wealthy woman had reviled her. She returned home empty handed, with tears and mutterings, and related to her husband the zaddik all that the wife of the gevir had done to her.

The rabbi immediately dispatched his shammash to the gevir, that he might return the fish, since the man's wife had grabbed the fish unjustly from the rebbetzin's hands after she had paid for them. Instructing the shammash also to tell the wife of the gevir that she was an evil woman and an adulteress.

The shammash pleaded with the rabbi to free him of this errand,

- Do you know to whom you send me to say these things? It is the gevir of the city, and when his officers hear my words they will beat me mercilessly. How dare I go to the mayor's house and tell him that his wife is an adulteress? For they will drag me out and toss me into the gutter by my forelock, as if I were a mere scoundrel.

But the rabbi did not attend his heart to the shammash's remarks and said,

- It is I who am master here, and I command you to go on my errand and say these things in my name. What can they do to you? For it is your duty to do all I bid you.

The shammash said to Rabbi Abraham Yehoshua Heschel,

- What can I do? I go unwillingly, knowing that the gevir will not be silent even in honor of your esteemed Torah. As he has behaved toward you and your wife, thus will he do to me.

Knowing that his rabbi was a unique zaddik of whom he was greatly in awe, he went to the house of the gevir, and he began by saying,

- Shalom, peace be unto you. The rabbi requests that you return the two fish to him, since the rebbetzin purchased them before your wife came to the fishermen's market. In addition, the fisherman caught the fish especially for his wife, and your wife did not behave honestly, scorning the rebbetzin and shaming her before the people.

When the wife of the gevir heard the words of the shammash her anger burned strong. She ran into her house blaspheming the rabbi and his wife before all the important people of the community who had come to consult with her husband on various matters. She reviled and insulted the very names of their rabbi and rebbetzin, until the people could no longer bear to listen.

The shammash also could not bear it and he said to those present,

- All you gentlemen gathered here are witness that I must attend to the discipline of the community. I have been directed to obey to the words of the Chief Rabbi, Rabbenu D'mata. All things he instructs me, I will do, for he transmits his words through me; therefore, do not cast your anger upon me when I say here what my rabbi instructed. This is the responsibility of my position.

All the people agreed,

- Say your piece and do not fear, for this is the purpose for which we appointed you shammash of the community. You must obey our rabbi in all things.

The shammash continued,

- The rabbi commanded that I say before all those present here that this woman, the wife of the gevir, is an adulteress.

Thereupon, he slipped quickly out the door for fear of standing in that house one minute longer, certain that the gevir's family would beat him.

The Jews were amazed, and when the lady of the house heard these things, she began to shout and to wail,

- I told you what kind of man this rabbi is, and now you have heard him.

Thrown into alarm, the gevir's shamed heart brought flame into his countenance. For a time he sat dumb and confused, then he opened his mouth,

- Shall I stay silent before the man who has shamed my children. Therefore, before the onset of this Shabbat day, I declare that Rabbi Abraham Yehoshua Heschel's foot may not be set on any part of the city. And now, consult among you as to how to handle my decision, lest I let loose all my wrath upon his head.

This is how the gevir spoke, doubling and tripling the force of his intention.

The leaders of the community gathered in the house of the gevir were also very angry. They believed that their rabbi would not have made so bold as to dispatch such a message to the house of the gevir if he did not know the facts for certain. Nevertheless, they were confused. They believed the rabbi, yet they did not. All met outside the home of the gevir, consulting about what to do.

Then they returned to the gevir and said,

- Be moderate in your thoughts lest we risk being scorned. Let us cast our rabbi out of the city only after the holy

Informal study group - I. Moscowitz

Shabbos has gone. Wait until the morrow. On Shabbos, before the reading of the Torah, all the people will gather in the meeting house. Then, we will send for the rabbi and hear what he has to say, for the honor of our spiritual leader is precious to us and must not be scorned. If Rabbi Heschel does not regret and repent his words, we will denounce him before all the community. Then all will know that we have behaved moderately in this matter.

The gevir agreed to wait until the following day, but his wife began to scream bitterly that they must not; the rabbi must be thrown out of the city immediately. But the people did not attend to her words, and said,

- Wait until the morrow and we will see how the matter falls.

On Shabbos, after the Shacharit prayer, all the Jews gathered together in their meeting house. And it was the custom that the rabbi would remove the Torah Scroll from the Holy Ark and deliver a homiletic sermon of admonition taught from chapters of the Torah, in order to influence their hearts. Only after that would the members of the community speak or this and that. On that Shabbos, all the people departed from the synagogue and gathered together. Then the shammash was dispatched to inform the rabbi that all the people awaited him, and the gevir came also.

Rabbi Abraham Yehoshua Heschel walked there without removing the tallit from his shoulders, as was his custom after prayer service. Thus wrapped in the spirit of holy communication with the Almighty, he entered the meeting house. At the head of the table in the community room there was a special chair for the rabbi where no one else ever sat. But on that Shabbat, the gevir sat himself in the rabbi's chair. And the people agreed that they would not rise in respect when the rabbi entered the room. This would be the first sign that the rabbi was to leave their city.

But when the rabbi entered the building, a spirit of awe

246

fell upon the people and they all rose in respect before him, except for the gevir. A great trembling had taken hold of that one and he was struck dumb, and by reason of his distress he was unable to rise. The rabbi pushed him from the chair without saying a word. Then Rabbi Abraham Yehoshua Heschel of Aphta sat himself down at the head of all those gathered there, and said,

- My brothers, what is the need that caused you to gather here and what do you want of me?

And all the people replied,

- Yesterday, the rabbi sent a message saying that the wife of the gevir is an adulteress. We did not know and we did not ever see such a thing. For this reason, the rabbi must clarify the matter. For if not, how is it that he has declared the mother of the gevir's children to be an adulteress.

Then the rabbi spoke before them,

- I will prove this to you with clear and correct vision. But not on this day. I will not perform acts forbidden by Rabbinical Law on the Sabbath, for it is not permitted to sit in judgment on this day. Tomorrow will be sufficient time for this and all of you will be witness that there is no lie on my lips.

The community leaders were silent, but the gevir, husband of that woman poured his wrath upon them,

- Why are you listening to his foolish prattle? It he can prove such a thing, let this day witness it. The matter is permitted today, and this man speaks nonsense. I will tell you the true intention of the rabbi. He wishes to escape the city under cover of night. Tomorrow you will search him out and not find him and this is how he will prove his words, because the one to question will be gone.

The rabbi set his eyes on him in anger and the gevir fell dumb. Then the rabbi spoke,

- Be silent, fool! Do not speak idiot words of mischief. I will not lie to those who have placed their trust in me, G-d

247

forbid. And you, on the morrow, know that humiliation awaits you . . . But truth to tell, the fault is not with you, since you had no knowledge of this. Now, if you wish, I will explain how we will clarify this matter on the morrow. For the man who has committed this sin with your wife will come and bear witness before the entire community. He will relate how it happened, and she, your wife, will admit the truth. Tomorrow, all will know for certain.

The rabbi called the shammash to approach him and said,

- Tomorrow morning, take my staff to the cemetery and go to the grave of this certain man. Knock on the grave with the staff, calling out, "Such and such person! The rabbi hereby calls upon you to come to him in the third hour of this day." At that hour, all the Jews will gather in this place, and also the adulteress must be here. Then all the people will know that there is an Almighty Judge in Israel.

But the rabbi cautioned the shammash to hang a small dividing curtain between the spirit who had been summoned and the people of the community, so that a separate space was set aside for the dead soul. Then he said,

- My people, come and gather in this place tomorrow, all of you, and be seated at the table. Then you will see scenes and hear wonders.

On the morrow, all the Jews of the town gathered together in the meeting house, the men and the children and the women with babes in arms, to witness the circumstance which the rabbi would bring about there. The rabbi donned tefillin and prayed the shacharit prayer. In the third hour of the day, Rabbi Abraham Yehoshua Heschel of Aphta proceeded to the meeting house and took his place in his chair,

- Send for the woman!

But she refused to come, cursing and blaspheming the rabbi and the shammash. So the rabbi sent for her a second time, saying,

- If you do not attend the meeting house, I will dispatch the dead man to seek you out and transport you against your will. If that happens, I cannot say if you will be brought here alive or dead, because once permission is granted to the "great destroyer", he does not differentiate.

Thereupon, the woman accompanied the shammash. Then the rabbi declared,

- Jews of my community, would you recognize the voice of a man who died not long ago, the scribe employed at the house of this gevir.

And they all said,

- Yes, we well know his voice.

Then the rabbi said,

- You will not be able to observe the dead man, since that would cause mortal fear to fall upon you and bring you harm. Therefore, you will only hear his voice. He is here among us – behind the curtain.

The rabbi instructed that the curtain be lifted a bit. Then he said to the deceased,

- You are such-and-such. Now, please tell the people gathered here how this matter of the adultery came about between yourself and this woman.

A voice emerged from behind the curtain,

- Listen my brethren and my people. I was ensnared in this woman's net when I was a faithful of the gevir's house and in charge of his account books. One day, the gevir traveled on business to the city of Bucharest and I was in his house perusing the accounts. The lady instructed that I must come to sleep that night in her house, saying that she was frightened to be there alone. And I did not think a wanton thought for one moment. I truly believed that she was afraid to remain in her house without her husband. So, that night I came to sleep there and I lay down in the accounts room where the money is kept. The lady went to sleep in the

249

bedroom a far distance from there, at the other end of the house.

In the middle of the night, the lady walked through the four rooms which separated us, and came to where I was sleeping. She lay down next to me and when I awoke, alarmed, and asked,

- Who is this?

She said to me,

- I am the lady of the house and I have come to you so that you should satisfy my passion. For this, I will make you a very wealthy man. But if you refuse me, your end will be bitter. Then I will broadcast the lie that you stole money from the gevir and I will cause you to be cast into prison. Therefore, embrace and kiss me and promise me all good things.

- This is how I fell, like a deer in the net, not once and not twice. And now, woe is to me and aya! For this, I have lost Eden and my eternal life in the world of truth. My fellow Jews, decide what my judgment must be for this sin. For I did not restrain my desire.

The dead soul continued to weep before the people who sat silently and he told of his perpetual suffering in the torturous hollow of the sling, where he was cast repeatedly from one end of creation to the other. There was no rest, for even Gehenna was closed to him. He told of all the terrible things that had befallen him from the day he left this world until that moment, and all the people began to lament for him and weep.

Only then did the rabbi raise his voice and say,

- Evil woman, admit that these events are true and that this dead soul tells truth in the testimony which he has declared before you today.

The woman was fallen mute as a dove. Again, the rabbi admonished her, after which she raised her voice in weeping,

- I cannot deny the words of the dead soul, because they are truth.

Then the rabbi said,

- Now all here know, with the help of the Almighty, that no lie has passed my lips.

The Rabbi ordered that a scribe and witnesses be brought before him. He drew up a legal divorce for the gevir from to the adulteress. Then the rabbi instructed the woman in a severe discipline of penance, that she might repair her damaged soul.

As for the deceased spirit, Rabbi Heschel appointed and devised an exceptional remedy, because he had performed the difficult repentance of admitting his sin before all the company who until this time had not known and considered him an honest man.

The end of the tale was that Rabbi Abraham Yehoshua Heschel was honored and all the people of the town were strengthened in their certainty of the wondrous quality of their rabbi.

He did not linger in the city of Jassi. Soon, he went to serve as the Presiding Judge of the Bet Din of Aphta. And he went on to serve the Jews of the city of Medzibezh.

Remove the Evil Edict

The ruler of Galicia issued a very harsh edict which cast all the Jews into dire dread. The bet midrash of Rabbi Elimelech, of blessed memory, was in the Galician town of Lyzhansk. In this study hall every day of the week a most excellent Torah scholar by the name of Reb' Faivel would sit with diligence to study the holy books. A pure and forthright G-d fearing man, late one night this same Reb' Faivel visited the house of Rabbi Elimelech, called the "No'am Elimelech", according to the name of a scholarly work which he had authored, saying to him,

- Rabbi, I have a Torah litigation to submit to you: The Blessed Almighty has declared, "All the Children of Israel are bondsmen - for they serve and worship me." If this is so, then how can we take upon ourselves to be bondsmen to the Emperor and his inhumane decrees, and we are already servitors to the Lord of the Universe?

His Rabbi replied:

- These are wise words which you speak; however, one does not litigate during the night hours.

The next morning Rabbi Elimelech was visited by three learned Gaonim. They were the Maggid of Kojznitz, the Rabbi of Lublin and Rabbi Abraham Yehoshua Heschel of

Apftah. Rejoicing in his guests, he invited them to share his repast. During the meal the Rebbe Elimelech called upon Reb' Faivel to come before them.

The Rabbi, of blessed memory, said to him,

- Present to my colleagues the Torah litigation which you brought before me last night.

In awe of the great rabbis seated there, Reb' Faivel hesitated,

- Now, I have lost my enthusiasm in this matter.

But his Rabbi encouraged him,

- I ask that you speak of this matter. Tell us what you spoke of last night.

The three Gaonim heard him out, attending to the details of his plea. When he concluded, the first to speak was Rabbi Abraham Yehoshua Heschel.

- After we have heard the arguments of a litigation it is customary to ask the involved parties to leave the room so that we can discuss the case. You, therefore, Reb' Faivel will leave the room. But how can we ask the Lord of the Universe to leave our presence when it is His glory which fills all of creation? In addition, each and every one of our successful enterprises is due only to the fact that the Almighty always accompanies us, though we be defiled and less than pure!

- Notwithstanding this difficulty, Reb' Faivel, I can assure you that justice will not be compromised in your Torah litigation. We will examine all sides of the issue and arrive at a true solution.

Following the meal, the three Gaonim sat together to study the controversy, by creed and by canon. What should be the just decision? Could the Emperor impose an ill-contrived decree of this nature which would be injurious to every Jewish man, woman and child, in the manner so well pointed out by Reb' Faivel? This seemed in truth to be "an edict the people can not endure", which in Jewish law is a strict guideline according to which a law may either be adopted or rejected.

For long hours they debated and argued the Law well, searching out solutions in the "Hoshen Mishpat", one of the four volumes contained in the important halachic work the Shulchan Aruch, and many other sources.

Their conclusion was that Reb' Faivel's claim was just. And they recorded this judgment.

Within three days of this Torah litigation and the verdict of the Gaonim, the Almighty caused the Emperor of Galicia to cancel his malicious decree. An announcement was published throughout the land that the evil edict had been annulled.

This narrative is an example of how the merits of the learned zaddikim protected and preserved our people throughout their long exile.

This World
and the World
to Come

I n the city of Austraha lived two men, business partners who loved each other dearly all the days of their lives. Once, they learned that a certain Duchess, not experienced in merchandising, had acquired an inheritance of hundreds of rolls of fine fabric. And they wished to purchase this fabric at a cheap price.

The partners journeyed to the Duchess's manorhouse and approached the house steward, saying,

- Two Jews have come to purchase all the material from the Duchess at a good and fair price. The Duchess had never seen the face of a Jew, for she resided in a province of Russia where there were no Israelites. The Jewish people were strange to her and she did not wish to permit one to enter her home, or to meet with these two men at all. Also, she had never dealt in business and did not know how to bargain. But since she wished to sell the fabric, she decided upon a price through the trustee of her estate, who negotiated with the Jewish partners. They paid him and were free to take their merchandise.

When her trustee had brought the money to her hand, she questioned him regarding the quality of these Hebrews, since her forefathers had told her that they were robbers and wrongdoers and filled with deceit. Had they not murdered the messiah of the Christian people?

Her trustee said to her,

- What your forefathers told you is a lie. The Jews are trustworthy in their business dealings. Like all other folk, there are holy men among them and there are unjust men among them.

When the Duchess heard these words, she was desirous of seeing their faces and went to the entrance of her house to have a look. Seeing that one partner was very handsome, and admiring his extremely fine looks, she sent for this partner. When they spoke and she heard him turn a good phrase in her own tongue, she took even greater pleasure in him. After this, she began to burn with love for him and soon fell ill with it. Meanwhile, the partners delayed in her court for several days, measuring the fabric and hiring wagons for transport.

One day prior to leaving that place, observing that the wagons hired were not sufficient, the older partner traveled to the nearby city to hire additional wagons. The younger, handsome one, remained at the manor to load the material onto the wagons. When the Duchess learned that the favored partner had remained at the manor she sent for him and revealed her love sickness.

But the man did not yield to her, whereupon, she offered to return to him the payment for sale of the fabric, only that he might do her will. Soon, his passions took hold of him, and also avarice for the money she gave. And that night he was tempted and succumbed to her will. When, at daybreak he came to tend to the merchandise, his partner had already arrived with the additional wagons. Loading the remaining fabric onto the wagons, they set out happily and of good cheer on their return journey.

Along their way, the handsome partner could not put out of his mind what he had done and what had taken place. Sad of heart, he deeply regretted his actions and began to sigh mournful sighs. His partner asked,

- Why has your face fallen? Thanks be to the Lord, we have purchased merchandise at a very cheap price, even better than we imagined. With G-d's help, we will make a fine profit from this fabric. So what are these sighs?

The younger partner put him off with various excuses. However, when he did not cease to groan and sigh, his friend pleaded that he explain the meaning of it; for he understood that it was no small matter and not for nothing was his friend saddened. Thereupon, he disclosed all that had transpired with the Duchess. In addition, he told his friend that they had actually purchased the fabric for nothing, showing him the money the Duchess had returned to him. He greatly regretted this and was very troubled, but his partner ridiculed him,

- With such an amount of ma'ot you can perform much charity and mitzvot. You know that repentence repairs all sins.

His partner would not be comforted, and he wept much for what he had done. When his friend saw this, he said,

- If I purchase this transgression from you, what will you give me?

When the man heard his partner's offer he did not tarry,

- Take all the ma'ot that I received from the Duchess, and I will add to it a quarter of my share of the fabric.

The older partner said,

- We shared in the merchandise, and shall share in the transgression; let us divide the money evenly.

But the younger refused, saying,

- If you wish to take my sin upon yourself, I will give you

259

Chasidim Dancing

all the material and I do not wish even part of the merchandise for the money I received from the Duchess.

This offer aroused the older partner's avarice, and he agreed,

- Let it be as you say.

They shook hands between them. And the older partner thus purchased the younger's transgression in a one-hundred percent legitimate transaction.

When they returned to their city, Austraha, the buyer of the sin sold his merchandise, earned much money and became a very wealthy man. But it was not long before he passed on from this world. When he came before the celestial court of judgement to present account for the actions of his life, among his own transgressions was counted the sin committed by the younger partner with the Duchess. But the man complained,

- This thing never happened to me!

And the celestial court asked him,

- Have you not purchased this transgression from your partner?

- But, why should I be punished for a sin I did not perform, for I only took the money!

After much haggling over this and that he was permitted to appear before a Torah judgment together with his partner.

Thus it was that the dead man appeared to his partner in a dream and invited him to a Torah judgment. The younger partner became very terrified and did not know what to reply. However, the dead man did not rest or cease his efforts, coming to his former partner in a dream night after night and demanding that he join him in judgment. Until the live partner fell ill.

The Presiding Judge of the Bet Din of Austraha at that time was the Gaon and Zaddik Maharsha, Rabbi Samuel Eliezer Ben Judah Ha-Levi Edels, of blessed memory, one of the greatest commentators on the Talmud. The sick man implored his family to carry him on his bed to the home of the great rabbi. There he wept profusely and related to him the entire incident, from its beginning to its end.

- And now, I am to die. Every night my dead partner comes to me in a dream, demanding that I stand trial. Rabbi, advise me how to behave before the celestial court.

The Maharsha, of blessed memory, replied and said,

- Do not fear. Go to your home and when the dead man next comes to you, tell him in my name that the Torah is in this world and the Torah court of this world is of importance as well. Therefore, if he wishes to appear in Torah judgement with you, let him come and stand before me. If he refuses, tell him that he must leave you in peace or I will excommunicate his soul.

The sick man did as he was instructed. When the dead man came to him, he repeated the words of the Maharsha and on that night the deceased let the sick man be. But soon he returned again in a night dream, saying,

- Come with me before the Maharsha.

Then the sick man requested,

- Wait until my health has returned to me and then I will stand trial with you.

The deceased allowed the sick man thirty days to return to health. After one month's time, they would appear before the Torah court of the Maharsha.

Time passed and the sick man recovered. He went to the Maharsha and said that on a certain day he must stand up against the dead man before the court. The Maharsha instructed his shammash that all the community be gathered there on that very day and be taught a lesson in morals. A special area would be set aside for the deceased soul at the bet midrash so that the dead not mix with the living and cause harm.

On the day of the trial, the Maharsha dispatched the shammash to the cemetery to the grave of the deceased and called him to the trial. And so they came, the deceased and the live partner, and all the people gathered in the bet midrash. Then the live partner declared before the Maharsha as follows, relating the entire incident from its beginning to its end,

- I have regretted my actions and I have wept and wept. For had my dead partner not purchased the transgression from me, I would have repented and attended your honor, the rabbi, that you might teach me all manner of repentance. But when my partner purchased and took upon himself the transgression, when he accepted all the money which I was given by the Duchess for performing this sin, to which I also added my share of the purchase, I believed in my heart that no sin applied to me at all. And why has he come now to me to terrify and grieve me with his demand and his calumny?

And the live partner addressed the deceased directly,

- For you purchased the transgression from me in a full and correct transaction. And we shook hands over this agreement!

When he had finished speaking, the dead man began his side of the claim, saying,

- True, it was folly of me to purchase your sin, but I only did so to calm your sorrow. And it is true that I did not imagine matters to end in this way. I always intended to return the ma'ot to you and the incident be forgotten. As for you, I may owe you money, but am not liable to be punished for your sin. How can I be punished for a sin which I myself did not enjoy, for it is you who commited this sin? Must I be flogged for your sake?

And throughout the duration of that court judgement, the deceased was not visible. A partition was hung between him and the living. Thus, the living partner and the deceased continued to speak their claims before the Maharsha until there was no more to say. And the Maharsha said,

- The words of the live partner are more just than those of

the deceased partner, since by reason of the latter's behavior the live partner was prevented from seeking repentance until this time. A deal remains a deal, a price is a price and a fool remains a fool. For was it not sufficient unto the deceased that he himself was not drawn into such a sin. He did not thank the Almighty for saving him from transgression, but went and purchased foreign sins to heap onto those already in his baggage.

When the dead man heard these words, he raised his voice in high lament before all the people, and cried out,

- I hoped that my claim would prove just. For my partner is alive and he can still repent. But what can the dead do? And woe to me, for I am not permitted to stand in this place one moment longer. The celestial court calls to me, saying,

- Your judgment has already been passed by the holy rabbi.

Now, the Maharsha did comfort the deceased, saying that he would perform a tikkun for his soul and ask that the harsh penalty be lightened a degree. And the rabbi would teach the way of repentance to the live partner in order that his punishment be eased. But the decision was sealed. Justice was with the live partner.

When the rabbi ceased to speak, the people heard a loud sound of great weeping. From the place where the dead man had spoken, a great mist rose up and his spirit was taken.

Tenth for a Quorum

A true story of a time that Rabbi David of Miklayev was journeying to be beside the Ba'al Shem Tov on Yom Kippur. It was his habit in sacred matters to be in Medzibezh for the High Holy Days – from the eve of Rosh HaShanah until after Yom Kippur day. But that year, Rabbi David was prevented from traveling before Rosh HaShanah and he was very sorry about this. Therefore, he made preparations in great haste to arrive on Yom Kippur Eve. On that day, he experienced many delays until he was forced to set out on his journey after the noon hour had come and gone.

Near to the city of Medzibezh he passed through a small village where several Jews resided. Seeing a Jew hurrying through their village they ran to halt his wagon, calling out that a Jewish man was needed to complete the obligatory minyan of ten for their Yom Kippur prayer service.

- Honorable rabbi, please tarry and pray with us.

Knowing well the important mitzvah of completing a quorum, Rabbi David wished to comply. But he considered and estimated the great degree of travail and trouble he had endured, and how much devotion he had expended to enjoy the privilege of being in the company of the Ba'al Shem Tov on Yom Kippur day. Now that he was so close, would he not be there? So he replied,

- I will not be able to tarry with you; I am in a great hurry and must complete my journey.

Ordering the wagon driver to spur the horses on, they raced forward to Medzibezh. When he arrived, the Besh't was in the midst of Minchah prayer, and the zaddik did not greet him or say a word to him.

After Yom Kippur day was over, the Besh't blessed Rabbi David without warmth and showed no signs of intimacy as was his usual and profound habit. This made Rabbi David very unhappy and he searched his own behavior for the cause. Perhaps the Ba'al Shem Tov had observed some sin in him, but he found nothing. Then a dread fell upon Rabbi David and a great fear that a certain personal act, judged honest in his own heart and thus not considered liable to himself, was not worthy. For he was not as yet skilled to define his own blame, to observe and judge his own actions from aside, as are the pure zaddikim.

Sunken in sorrow, he determined that he would remain with the Besh't during the Sukkoth holiday which followed. Then, he would ask that the Rebbe reveal to him the root of the matter. However, immediately following the Shabbat on which the Torah portion of Bereshit is recited in the synagogue, the Besh't called him over and said,

- Rabbi David, know that without intention you have murdered a soul, because in that village where they called on you to complete a minyan, a soul has been awaiting you this seventy years. This soul is a particle which once belonged to the roots of your own soul. And this Erev Yom Kippur, you were intended to pray in that place and perform a tikkun, permitting this particle to rise and join the holy sparks. When you abandoned that village, you caused the tikkun of that blemished particle of soul to be delayed. Now, in order to repent your trangression, obligate yourself to exile and thus bring about the tikkun marred by you.

Then Rabbi David said to the Besh't,

- Mechubadi, I stand ready to perform what you will instruct.

The Besh't said to Rabbi David,

- Accept exile. For now you must wander to and fro where no one knows you, and in the towns you traverse deliver sermons to support yourself. But, no matter where you go, you must introduce yourself as a simple darshan, not well versed in the wisdoms of the Torah.

- Until when will I be wanderer?

- You will know yourself the day you are to return home.

And Rabbi David did as had been dictated by the Besh't. He did not return to his home, but set out to wander from place to place in exile. From city to town did he roam, clothed in plain garb so that none should recognize him as Rabbi Rabbi David of Miklayev; since by that time Rabbi David was reknowned as a devout and excellent Torah scholar. Thus, altered in manner and costume, no man knew him.

Two years and a half passed. At that time, Rabbi David arrived at one of the large cities in Lithuania by the name of Slonim. There he was hosted at the home of the parnass and such was the custom, that morals preachers passing through the city were hosted by the Jewish community leader who took that task upon himself on that particular month. Having arrived there on the fifth day of Shabbos week. The parnass welcomed him and asked that he deliver some words of Torah from among his sermons. Rabbi David's words appealed very much to the parnass who said,

- If you choose, I will arrange for you to discourse on this week's Torah portion in the great synagogue of my city.

- I do not wish this. It is enough that I deliver a drasha in one of the smaller study halls.

- I do not agree, for it is unsuited to your scholarship. I ask that you deliver your sermon in the great synagogue.

At noon of the eve of the Holy Shabbos, a great excitement took hold of the Jews of Slonim, for an important rabbi-darshan had just arrived in the city to deliver his sermon. Immediately, the parnass went to greet him together with the townspeople. He brought this rabbi back to his house to prepare comfortable quarters for him and his party. They all spent the Shabbos together there, and Rabbi David among them.

On the Shabbat eve, as all were seated around the Shabbat table, the well-known darshan asked Rabbi David about himself. The parnass spoke for him, saying,

- This is a darshan who wishes to deliver a sermon in our city. In my opinion he is excellent, and were your learned self not here with us, I would allow him to deliver his sermon in the great synagogue. But now, Rabbi David will speak in the study hall on a day of the week. If he chooses to remain with us until the next blessed Shabbos, then he will be doresh in the great synagogue. While your learned honor will expound to the community on in the great synagogue of our city.

The well known darshan asked Rabbi David to deliver a homily, but he did not wish to do so. Humbling himself, he declared that he was not worthy. Finally, the darshan rebuked him,

- One does not refuse an important man such as myself!

So Rabbi David spoke several clumsy words of Torah and the darshan mocked him,

- Can this be considered a drasha?

And he laughed at the parnass who had praised Rabbi David,

- This is a totally ignorant man who knows not at all to expound Torah.

After this, the well-known darshan delivered his sermon, speaking words of Torah and morals and at the end of his

Paying homage to the Torah

words they drank wine in his honor. Rabbi David sat humbled at the foot of the table, and they extended no honor to him. The parnass fell asleep, and unable to waken him, his servants carried him to his bed. Too, all the guests lay sleeping and the Shabbos candles were soon extinguished.

Rabbi David lay himself on the floor of that same room which had been prepared for the darshan. And as was his custom from the time that he had taken himself into exile, he did not seek the comfort of sleeping in a bed with counterpane.

The household slept, except for the famous darshan whose passions were aroused. He imagined to himself that since the parnass was deep in the sleep of the drunkard, he would not know his wife tonight. Thus, the evil instinct tempted him, and he quietly approached the wife of the parnass. But, by virtue of the many people present in the house at that time, the transgression was prevented from him. When he came to the woman, she was aroused from her sleep and began to shout,

- Who are you? Tell me! Tell me!

Because she knew that her husband was sound asleep.

The scoundrel fell silent and tongue-tied as a dumfounded dove. The wife of the parnass, when she could no longer hold on to the transgressor, clutched the skullcap off his head and the man slipped from her grasp. All the members of the household began to awaken. The darshan hurried to his room and stole the skullcap from the sleeping Rabbi David. Placing it on his own head, he lay on his bed and spoke as though he had just now been wakened by the noise,

- What is this, oi what is this?

The servant heard the fuss and came to light candles so that all would see who was the cause of this evil. When candles were lit, the darshan bent over Rabbi David sleeping on the floor without head covering and without skullcap and kicked him in the foot,

- Troublemaker in Israel, may the Almighty make trouble for you!

Since Rabbi David said nothing, the darshan ordered that he be imprisoned and bound in the darkness. He was led to the guard room in the government house and they watched over him there.

On the next day, all the city wondered about this blasphemous act, and the corrupt darshan delivered his sermon on Shabbat in the great synagogue,

- The city is not clean, the proof being that such an outrageous act occured in the house of the parnass when I was in your city.

After the drasha was over, this sinful man ordered that the people gather together after the Holy Shabbos, immediately following the havdala service, so that they all should witness the sinner punished and thus be instructed in a moral lesson.

And so it was that all the Jews gathered after havdala, and Rabbi David was brought there and stood before them. His hands were manacled and the ungodly darshan showered morals upon him, his voice bellowing,

- Evil one, admit your perverted ways!

Rabbi David stood silent and said nothing. Then the darshan commanded that he be whipped with the lash until he would admit his sin. Therefore, was Rabbi David laid onto the ground, and the community beadles stood ready to punish him.

And here, a loud voice knocked gruffly at the window,

- Is Rabbi Rabbi David of Miklayev here?

All ran outside to see whose voice was hammering at the windows, but there was no man there. They wondered and they sent people to search around the house and see who it could be.

The voice ceased and soon all had calmed down. Again

they laid Rabbi David on the ground to whip him. And here again the voice sounded out, striking at all the window panes,

- Is Rabbi Rabbi David of Miklayev here?

They all ran out and behold there was no man, and all the people wondered exceedingly.

Then the darshan spoke,

- This is nothing more than Rabbi David's scorcery, by bewitchment has he done all this. We will flog him with whips until he admits his sin.

They laid Rabbi David on the ground a third time, but again the voice spoke, this time saying,

- But it is truly Rabbi Rabbi David of Miklayev. And why are you silent and say nothing?

Then Rabbi David replied,

- And what shall I shout? For I am here to bear my punishment and be redeemed from my sins.

The people were very surprised, since all knew the name of Rabbi Rabbi David of Miklayev, that he was a great man. They let him be, consulting together. Was this man really Rabbi Rabbi David, so well-known at the gates? Recalling that in their city resided two men who had seen Rabbi David in the house of the zaddik, the Ba'al Shem Tov, they sent for them that they might declare whether this man was the very same.

The two men came to that place and knew him, falling on their faces and weeping,

- What has happened to you, rabbenu?

Rabbi David replied,

- I am not guilty of this crime which occured in the house of the parnass. But rather the Besh't declared me into exile until the day that I would be permitted to reveal my name. When the voice called out from the heavens, asking, "Why are you silent?" I recalled that the Besh't had said: "From your own self will you know the time that your transgression has been forgiven."

- I see that this time has come. And now, I must reveal that it was this darshan who crept to the wife of the parnass in the night. When she pulled his skullcap from his head, he came and stole my own skullcap. The sign of proof is that beneath the lining of the cap he wears is sewn a kamea which I keep on my head at all times. Please, look and you will see if my words are correct.

Immediately they removed the scullcap from the head of the darshan, tore open the lining and were proven that the kamea was there.

All the punishments intended for Rabbi David were heaped on to the sinful darshan. As is written in Proverbs, "The righteous is delivered out of trouble, and the wicked comes in his stead."

The Modest Will Be Granted Hidden Wisdoms

Rabbenue Moshe Lieb Isserles, the Rema, had one friend since the days of his early youth with whom he had studied in heder. It was no other than Rabbi Haim ben Reb' Bezalel, the brother of the Holy Maharal of Prague, all now of late and blessed memory. These friends, Rabbenu Moshe and Reb' Haim were always together in love and wonderful affection.

When Rabbenu Isserles was accepted to serve as Rabbi and Presiding Judge of the Bet Din in Cracow, his soul-comrade and friend Reb' Haim acompanied him. It was agreed between them that when Rabbenu Moshe must journey to the outlying Jewish villages to sit in judgment, Reb' Haim would serve the community in Cracow and deliver his learned responses to Jews approaching the court. And when The Rema would serve the Cracow Bet Din, Reb' Haim would travel and govern Jews in the cities of the northern region in Torah law.

The unhappy day came that the wife of Reb' Haim passed away. After the proper interval had passed, all the city began to fuss and seek out marriage proposals for Reb' Haim with daughters of prestigious gevirim and rabbis. But no one was good enough in the eyes of Rabbenu Moshe, since he well knew the great quality of his friend. When the matchmakers saw that Rabbenu would not choose a wife for Reb' Haim, they ceased to speak with him in this matter.

After a year had passed that Reb Haim was without a wife and he never said a word regarding marriage, the matchmakers understood that Reb' Haim depended on Rabbenu Moshe to choose the suitable match for him. But truth to tell, Reb' Haim did not think this at all.

Once when his comrade had departed to the northern cities, Reb' Haim sent for a matchmaker whom he knew to be a sage and a discreet man,

- Listen to what I say, but conceal it from all men. Find a match for me in this city in the manner which I will instruct you. Seek out a modest woman from a humble and a kosher family. Her father must have a special room in his courtyard where I will sit and learn. For this, I need many books, and my father-in-law must be able to support me so that I can devote myself to study deeply in the Torah. And I will agree to such a match only if the father will not reveal to any man that I am the husband of his daughter. If you find a man to suit all these conditions, I will tell you what to do.

The shadchan asked about the city and finally decided on a certain Jewish baker whom he knew to be a kosher man. He went to him and said,

- Listen to me, my brother. All the days of your life you never imagined such a success as I bring you now. A blessing to you and your sons after you if you accept the great rabbi, Rabbenu Haim as husband to your daughter. I know that you are a pure and honest man, a baker occupied in his trade in good faith, and you have a decent and kosher daughter. So this is what you must do, for Reb' Haim has said this and this to me. Beware not to reveal this matter, and do zealously what I say, since soon Rabbenu Moshe will return from the northern cities and we will be prevented from discussing this matter further.

The baker agreed,

- I am ready and prepared to bring this wondrous scholar into my home and to give him my daughter as wife. I have a room far from the bustle of the city, but I have no books. Take these two thousand gold coins and ask the rabbi what books to purchase that I may place them in the room in the courtyard of my house. I pray that the blessed Almighty will grant you skill to complete what you have begun. And all for the best.

The shadchan returned home happily, knowing that the baker would pay him a good fee for his efforts. Reb' Haim said that the matter was to his approval and wrote down a list of books which the matchmaker purchased and brought into the special room. All was conducted in great secret. The baker agreed not to speak of it to any person, not even after the wedding. At the drawing up of the betrothal agreement only the rabbi, the baker and the shadchan were present. Then Reb' Haim said that when the Rema returned from his journey, he would see how the matter fell.

When Rabbenu Moshe returned and asked after the health of his friend Rabbenu Haim, he embraced him and saw that the face of his friend was dark with consternation. And he asked,

- My friend and comrade, why are you disturbed? Is there a matter lacking in me, or does your soul grieve because you have no wife? Then know that soon your release from loneliness will come. While in the northern cities, I was offered a match for you with the daughter of the chief rabbi of a certain city. The matter remained in my heart and if you wish it, I write a letter and the father will travel here to seal the matter in the best way.

Reb' Haim hesitated and was silent.

When two days passed, Reb' Haim said to Rabbenu Moshe,

- Know my friend, that I have decided to travel to my family, to the house of my father in Prague. Although you are better to me than ten brothers, still my heart is restless and longs to see my family and my elder brother, the Maharal of Prague.

Rabbi Moshe's eyes welled with tears,

- Would you do this to me? You know that my soul is linked to yours, that you are more precious in my eyes than ten sons. What is lacking for you here with me? Cease to speak of these matters which make my soul unhappy. For all the days of my life, I will not allow you to part from me.

Then Rabbi Haim also wept and was silent and said not a word.

But, after a time he said,

- My friend and comrade, please do not speak again thus, because I will alter nothing of what I have said. My heart is not at rest and longs for my family and the house of my father. I also want to earn the great mitzvah of honoring my elder brother. Do not murmur against me as the parting from you lies heavy on my heart. But what am I to do? My mind is set on it.

When Rabbenu saw that he was firm in his decision and that all his words would not change it, he wept and said,

- If your decision is made, allow me to extend you honor before you part from me. Therefore, on the following blessed Rosh Hodesh day, I will hold a great feast in your honor. Then I will send you off with great tribute as is your due.

These words were good to Reb' Haim and sadly he made ready to part from his friend, saying

- I see that I have found favor in your eyes.

Reb' Haim returned to his Torah and his work, and no oneknew the secrets of his thoughts and plans for the

278

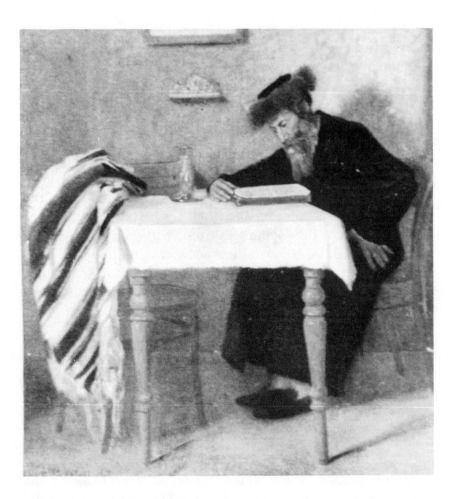

Private Study

coming days, except for two in his city – the shadchan and the baker.

On the blessed day of Rosh Hodesh, The Rema arranged a great feast for all the elders of the city. He hired a fine carriage and attendants to see Reb.' Haim along his way, but Reb' Haim refused them and chose only the trusted shadchan to accompany him. All the elders of the community, and also the baker who was to be his father-in-law, crowded round the carriage to give honor to the sagacious talmid hahkam now departing their city. And the Rema traveled part of the way with his beloved friend.

About two miles along their way, Rabbenu fell upon the shoulder of his comrade and they kissed and wept many tears in parting. the Rema returned to the city with all his entourage and the baker and shadchan remained with Reb' Haim and they traveled together along the road leading to Prague.

Before evening they came to one village where Reb' Haim dispatched the wagon-driver to his home, saying,

- The way is very long until I reach the city of my destination. In each district that I travel I will hire another carriage, until I reach my country and the land of my birth.

That night Reb' Haim altered his dress and appearance beyond recognition. He and the shadchan hired a local wagonner to return them to the city of Cracow near the midnight hour.

In the second watch, they arrived at the house of the baker, there they sent for seven simple country folk who did not know Reb' Haim. A wedding canopy was readied and the ceremony held. Then Reb' Haim sanctified his wife according to Jewish law. The wedding feast was held in the company of these seven country men who before the sunrise returned to their home. And the matter did not become known at all, except for the news that the baker had taken a groom for his daughter and he had not invited

280

anyone to the wedding feast as was usual and the custom. All his friends wondered at this, but with time the matter seemed forgotten.

From that day and for several years, Reb' Haim did not leave the threshold of his new home, studying with great diligence all the day and all the night. He allowed few hours for sleep and only his wife and father-in-law knew of his life. The days went by until two years had passed.

At that time, a plague fell upon the city of Cracow, Lord have pity on us, and the Jews of the city came to the Rema to search out and ask whether they had been guilty of a sin which brought about this unusual death. The rabbi's attendants went to clarify in the city, after which they returned to tell the rabbi,

- There is rumor that, these two years, a certain man resides in the house of the baker and he is suspect of living without hupa and kedushin with the man's daughter.

Rabbi Moshe Isserles replied,

- Bring this man me.

The rabbi's attendants went to the house of the baker and brought the man to the Cracow Bet Din where the Rema sat in judgment. The people present did not recognize him, and Reb' Haim kept his face lowered.

Informed that the sinner had arrived and was present in the bet din, The Rema emerged from his room and, gazing at the man, he knew him. Taking Reb' Haim by the hand, he brought him quickly into his own chamber where he fell onto his friend's shoulder and greatly wept. After a while, he raised his eyes and behold, Reb' Haim was laughing. Then Rabbi Moshe said,

- Three things will I ask you. From what place did you come to the house of the baker? What is your sin of which they speak? Why and for what reason do you laugh?

Then Reb' Haim replied,

- First things first and last things last. When I was occupied

281

with you in Torah judgments, the burden of public life prevented me from occupying myself with Torah and prayer. And the latter was my most sincere wish. Therefore, I chose a place where I could devote myself to learning Torah and prayer without distraction. So, I called for a certain shadchan and instructed him to do my bidding. And so it was, and this is how my intention was resolved.

- Regarding your second question, what is my sin? I will tell you the truth. These two years I have been occupying myself with Torah day and night, and nothing is lacking from my life. Truely it is very good; my father-in-law supports me honorably, and my wife is a kosher woman who performs the wishes of her husband. Noting in my heart that my share was abundant, this caused me to become concerned lest I fall into the snare of pride, Almighty forbid such a thing! Therefore, I asked the Almighty, He who weighs the heart, to humble me. It is true that it was not my intention to be brought to such humiliation as this. But if the wish of the Holy One Hallowed Be His Name is such, it is suitable and I accept this suffering with love.

- As for why I laughed, I laughed because I saw you weep.

Then Rabbenu Isserles called on his attendants and said to them,

- What have you done? Leave this man be, for he is not the sinner.

Reb' Haim sat in the house of The Rema for two weeks time and was happy and extremely joyous with him. Then he returned to his home.

Time passed and Rabbenu, The Rema had a thought,

- My comrade fled from the honor which intruded on his Torah study and prayer. He sought humility. I will go secretly to where he lives and watch his ways and customs. I will observe his steadfastness in the Torah and in prayer, that I may learn a good measure from him.

Following the midnight watch, he and his shammash went

to the house of the baker and stood behind the window of the room where Reb' Haim was learning to hear his method and manner of study and prayer. And here, two voices were heard in the room and the words of learning were splendid and elevated. The wisdom and profound comprehension found great favor in his eyes. He stood there half an hour more and then he knocked on the door and said,

- Open. For it is I, Moshe Isserles.

The door opened, Rabbenu entered, and to his surprise Reb' Haim was seated there alone. There was no man with him. He asked,

- But I have heard the voices of two men learning Torah, and now I see that you are alone. Tell me who was the person learning Torah with you?

Reb' Haim remained silent.

Only then did Rabbenu say,

- I command that you tell me the truth of this enigma. Do not cloak the truth from me.

Then his friend replied,

- I speak because you have commanded me to reveal to you the hidden mysteries. Know that it is the Prophet Elijah, of blessed memory, who teaches me Torah.

When the Rema heard the words of his friend he grew faint. With a depressed spirit, he said,

- Please ask Elijah the Prophet in my name, "What has been my sin and how have I transgressed that I have not earned until this day the privilege of his revealing himself to me and receiving Torah from his lips?"

Thereupon the Prophet Elijah replied through Reb' Haim,

- This is what you must say to Rabbenu Moshe Isserles. The celestials cannot not bear great and expansive gestures. This is why it is not my custom to reveal myself to those who conduct their rabbinical post with a superior hand. The Rema is occupied in holy service, and the rabbinical burden heavy on his shoulders obliges him to behave grandly and with glory. Therefore, I do not wish to reveal myself to him and to trouble him in his tasks, in the labor of holy work with which he is occupied.

For it is true that I love the modest and retiring who walk humbly with their G-d, those whose good works are hidden from the eyes of man. Only to these do I reveal myself.

Live Joyfully with the Wife Whom thou Lovest

This is a true tale which occured in Fez, the large capital city under Almighty's heaven, in the year four thousand and five hundred of the Almighty's creation. In this city there was a very wealthy Gaon Rabbi who had three sons of marriagable age. The rabbi posed a "she'elat hahkam", a query for a wise scholar learned in the secrets of the Torah, regarding the future of his three sons and what would be their fortunes; in what city should he seek their life-mates? In response, he was sent a dream telling him that all three sons would have the most fortuitous lives. Two would marry girls from Fez, and the youngest, whose fortune would be greater than his two brothers, would find his wife in a far away place. And it was not revealed to the rabbi what city this would be.

In due time, the rabbi married off his two elder boys. The

match for the third son, then 15 years old, did not yet concern the rabbi. A year passed, then two, and the third son began to wonder why his father had left him aside and not entered him under the marriage canopy. But he was shy to speak of this, and envious of his brothers. They were raising families, but he felt abandoned and forgotten. Envy became jealousy, and then hatred.

Observing his youngest son's behavior, the father understood what he was feeling towards his brothers. Deciding that it was time to tell him of the "she'alat hakham", he explained that his youngest son's wife would come from a far away place, but in the dream solution sent to him, the name of the city had not been revealed.

After hearing his father, the youngest son began to wander the streets of the city like a sleepwalker, or one whose reason has left him. And he would say aloud,

- Where is my wife? Where is my life-mate?"

When the father learned that his son wandered the streets and people ridiculed him, it was very grievous to him.

One day the rabbi had an idea. He would ask one of the vagabond beggers to take his son along with him to another town where he was not known. And so it was. The rabbi had given them food for the journey, and after traveling through barren wastes for two days, they came to a settlement where no people could be found. A powerful surge of river overflowed and caused the shore to be carpeted with lush green grass onboth sides. They sat on the banks of the river resting from the travails of their journey, and partook of the afternoon meal.

As they sat at their leisure, a great eagle soared down and lifted the son of the rabbi up by the locks of his hair, carrying him on high and disappearing over the crescent rim of the earth. After a time, he released his captive and let him drop onto the roof of one house.

The force of the blows when he was dropped caused

almost all his limbs to come apart, and he fainted. After five or so hours he returned to consciousness, he looked about and saw that he was lying on the roof of a house. Feeling himself in pain, he rested for some time, until he heard a voice from the loft room. It was the sing-song nigun sound of Gemarra study. A Jew was learning and repeating the words of the Talmud, desirous of understanding the deepest meanings of our Sages. Then the youth understood that he had fallen onto the roof of an Israelite home. He called out,

- I am of Israel, an Israelite am I. For the sake of the Almighty, have pity and remove me from this place.

The door to the loft opened and a lovely girl emerged to see who was calling for help. This girl was the daughter of the rabbi of the city. Because her soul had longed for Torah, her father had built her a study room in the roof loft so that she might be able to sit there day and night and learn the Torah with diligence. This girl had so far refused all the marriage proposals offered her, for she sought a talmid hakham greater than herself in learning. But there was no such Torah scholar, one who could win her over and surpass her in brilliance.

Seeing the youth, she asked immediately,

- Are you familiar with this particular Gemarra problem which I study? And she showed him the Gemarra page.

He replied,

- Yes. This-and-this is the correct solution.

Hearing his response, she said in her heart, "This youth is the destination of my soul. Although weary from his great fall, still his wisdom is exceeding."

She went into the house to bring fragrant spices that he might inhale and his consciousness be fully revived. Then she prepared food and drink and after he partook and his health had been restored, they sat together to learn

A Wedding Scene - I. bella

Gemarra. He taught her and she sat before him as does disciple before his rabbi mentor.

On the next day, she asked him if he had a wife and he told her that he as yet awaited the coming of his mate as forecast for him in heaven. He related all that had taken place in the house of his father and of the "she'elat hakham" and the dream solution sent to his father. When she heard these things, she said to him,

- The matter appears resolved; that you are my mazal and to be my husband.

On his third day there, an elderly man came to the room and sat near the table where they were learning. He said to them,

- Until when will you sit thusly without the benefit of a canopy and wedding vows? Come and I will arrange everything for you as befits Jewish law. And they agreed.

Now the old man was none other than Elijah the Prophet who conducted the binding of their wedding vows by Jewish law and wrote their ketuba with his very hand. That very night the canopy was set up and the old man married this youth to the young woman according to the way of Israel. Then the Prophet Elijah was gone and departed from their view.

When the sun rose the next morning, the groom arose and doused his hands with water according to ritual. He washed his face and went out to the roof where again a great eagle swooped down and took him away. The eagle flew to Fez and cast him onto the the house of his father.

When the bride saw that her husband had disappeared, she fainted and was taken to her bed where she lay ill for three months. To all who spoke to her, she would cry out,

- Where is my husband, where is my husband?

Her father and mother did not know at all about what had taken place with the young man because she had not told anyone. The parents were very unhappy for their beautiful and learned daughter who lay in her bed and spoke a confusion of words.

As for the groom, when he saw that he had fallen and was returned to the house of his father, that his bride was lost from him and all that had passed seemed as a dream, he went mad. After that, he would sit at the entrance to his father's house and turn a dumb ear to all who questioned his groaning. For a long time, he spoke not a word.

It happened one day, as he sat at the entrance to his father's house, that three men who had a falling out between them came to the house of the rabbi that he might judge their problem according to the Torah. The groom son of the rabbi asked,

- What is the argument which has come between you?

- We are three brothers whose father has died and left us as inheritance a precious stone, a priceless gem. We come to your father, the rabbi, that he might rule according to halachah regarding this stone.

The rabbi's son asked them,

- What is the nature of this stone and what are its virtues, that you quarrel thus and fight amongst yourselves because of it?

Then they told him,

- This gem is extraordinary, since it has two qualities. If you place it in your mouth, you taste every dish you love; and if you rest the gem on your arm, on the very spot where a man lays his tefillin, you rise into the air and are transported to any place you desire.

The rabbi's son thought wisely and advised them thus,

- Fools!. The decision of my father will be that the eldest son must receive twice the share of second and third son. What is more, my father will judge that you must sell the stone and each take his share. And here lies the danger.

- What is the danger?

- In order to sell the stone, you will have to bring it to a craftsman who understands the value of such gems in order to decide its sale price. He will surely ask you, "From what place have you come and what is your name and what is the name of your father and your city?" After which he will inform the king's treasury and they will take the stone from you against your will, as is customary in this country. Especially in Fez, a city rife with injustice and violence in all matters connected to our Israelite brethren. My advice to you is that a quarrel is not to your benefit. If you sell the stone to me, I will pay you much more than its true value.

- What will you give us and what price is more than its value?

- For the price of the gem I will give you my share in the world to come. That is surely worth more than a stone which can be stolen by judges or by thieves. Whereas, no one can steal my share in the world to come from you.

They heard his words and consulted amongst themselves. After which they wrote out the bill of sale, giving him the stone for the cost of his share in the world to come and went on their way.

When they had gone, the son of the rabbi tested the first quality of the stone – to taste any food in the world. When that truth was proven, he put the stone on to his arm on the very spot where he lay tefillin. Immediately, he was lifted from the ground and flown far from his home. Below him he saw a very great city, the very same which held his bride. Then he said in his heart, "I will descend and rest a bit before the gates of the city." He did so, descending at the great river crossing this city, and there he sat on the river shore to rest.

As he was sitting, very happily with the gem he had purchased, looking at it and thinking many thoughts, a large bird swooped down and grabbed the stone from his hand, flying above and back into the firmament. You can imagine how this miserable youth was now sorrowed, how much tears he wept for the loss of this precious stone. He almost went mad and stoned himself to death. For now, he did not know how to find the home of his bride. By reason of his unhappiness he made a vow that from this day forward he would no longer learn Torah.

The end of it was that he entered the city and starved for bread until he found daily labor at an Israelite baking establishment. His work was, on the third day of each Shabbat week to go to the homes of Jews who wished to bake their Shabbat bread at the baker's oven. He would take their dough to the baker and return the baked challah to them on Erev Shabbat. He did his work faithfully, and made his living in this way.

Now, the daughter of the rabbi of that city, the bride of this lost youth, was with child. On the day that her mother understood this and thus believed that her daughter had been wanton, the heart was broken within her. Against her own will, she went to tell her husband that soon their daughter would give birth. What would they do and what would they say? Where would they hide their shame? When the rabbi heard this bad news, he collapsed and fainted from the excess of misery. His wife instructed the shammash that the rabbi was ill and could not sit in judgment in the bet din.

When her daughter's time came and she began the birth throes in great difficulty, the mother went to help her. After several hours, a baby boy was born, and immediately the house was filled with a luminescence. There being no clothing prepared for the infant, the rabbi's wife removed clothing from her own body to wrap him. And she went to tell her husband of the new born boy, and that the house had become filled with light.

On the eighth day, the prescribed day of the brit mila, the sages of the city came to ask after the health of the rabbi. As they were seated before him, the daughter of the rabbi sent her attendant to invite the sages to where she was lying. They went up the loft room and she said to them,

- Fellow Jews, you must take this child and circumcise him.

The sages gazed one at the other astonished. The daughter continued,

- The Almighty forbids that you think badly of this child, lest you all be struck down with leprosy.

Immediately, the sages saw that leprosy had tainted their skin.

After the wife of the rabbi saw that her daughter's curse had come to be, she went to tell her husband. Only then did the rabbi agree to see his daughter. Rising before her father in respect, the daughter opened her wooden chest and revealed her ketuba, written by the very hand of Elijah the Prophet, of blessed memory. And then the learned girl related all that had befallen her, the sages listening to this wonder and amazement. After this, the rabbi asked that his daughter free them of the leprosy, and so it was; their flesh became smooth as that of a small child.

They performed the brit mila, and the day was a celebration for all. The important parnassim and learned Jews of the community came to bless them, and there was food and drink for the mitzvah feast. There never was such a joyous day as that one, by reason of the marvelous miracle they had witnessed with their own eyes. All the people of the town, when they heard this good news about the daughter of the rabbi and the child which had been born because of the blessing of Elijah the Prophet, were desirous to see the face of this child and his righteous mother.

The child grew and was weaned. One day, the baker's apprentice came to the rabbi's house to take the Shabbat dough for baking, and he saw the son of the daughter of the rabbi. Immediately, an excess of love burned within him. One moment he wept and the next he laughed. AFter that, whenever he saw the boy his countenance would alter, at times sad and then joyous. And he longed for this child in his heart, as if he were his own, and knew no peace in his soul. Soon, he began to frequent the rabbi's house more and more and to befriend this child, so beloved to him.

When the mother saw this, her heart began to clamor and cry out, "Why does the baker's apprentice behave in this way?" And she was very unhappy because she did not know the meaning of it. For why was the heart of this stranger drawn to her son. But she concealed her fear from all, and did not disturb the apprentice from amusing her child.

In that city there was one wealthy Jew who one day observed a gem, the size of a bird's egg, in a nest in the tree branches opposite his window. And the gem shone like the rays of the sun. So this wealthy gevir thought,

- Would that someone might climb the tree and bring me this nest.

He said to his wife,

- Call the baker's apprentice to here, that he might take down the nest and we will pay him for his labors.

On the next day, when the apprentice came to take the challah dough, the gevir said to him,

- If you will climb this tree and bring us the nest, we will pay you well for your effort.

The young man climbed the tree and in the nest, among the newly hatched eggs and fledgelings, he saw his very own gemstone. Secreting the gem in his bosom, he brought only the nest with fledgelings to the man who asked,

- What have you done? Why did you take the precious stone into your bosom?

- This stone belongs to me, therefore I have taken it.

They began to quarrel. One said, "The stone is mine," and the other said, "The stone is mine." Until the wife of the gevir took the stone by force from the young man's hand. She gave him several pennies for his effort and sent him from the house, closing the door behind him.

The young man went directly to the bet din and

demanded that this gevir be called to a Torah litigation. At the litigation, the rabbi asked the gevir,

- From whence has this stone come to you?

- It is an inheritance from my ancestors. And how could such a stone belong to the apprentice of a baker?

The conclusion was that the rabbi said that the stone certainly belonged to the gevir, and that since the apprentice took the trouble to bring it down with the nest, the gevir must only pay him half a gold coin for his trouble. When the young man saw that he had been dealt a false judgment, he went to tell the baker,

- I will never go again to the house of the rabbi to bring their challot, because the rabbi has judged me falsely. Please send another worker there.

And so it was, from that day forward, the apprentice distanced himself from the house of the rabbi and another brought the challot.

Two weeks passed and no one noted his absence, except for the daughter of the rabbi, who was very surprised when she saw that he had ceased to come and play with her precious son. And she asked her mother,

- Why is it that the baker's apprentice comes no more as was his custom?

But her mother did not know. Three days passed and the rabbi's daughter sent for the baker's apprentice to ask,

- It was lately your custom to visit us every day and to eat in our house. Why have three weeks passed that you do not come to us?

- The cause is such. I brought a certain matter before the bet din. But your respected father did not rule according to halachah.

She said to him,

- And if my father will judge you truly, then will you come to visit us?

- Certainly. For how can I not? Then, if you will it, I will visit to your house each and every day.

The daughter instructed him,

- Go to your work. Tomorrow I send for you and again there will be a din Torah. But this time, I will be present.

And so it was; the apprentice went on his way and the daughter of the rabbi went up to her loft room.

On that night, she dreamed a dream. She saw angels quarreling with one another. When she asked them, "Why is it that you quarrel?" they replied, "Why do you ask? Go to your father and say that in the matter of the baker's apprentice, he inclined his jugement unfairly in favor of the gevir."

The daughter arose and went to tell her father the words of the dream. And she said,

- My father, it is deserving that you investigate this matter well, for the truth of this judgment must be made clear.

In the morning, the rabbi invited the gevir and the apprentice to stand before him in din; and the daughter of the rabbi sat with them. The rabbi asked the gevir,

- The precious stone which the apprentice brought to you from the tree branches, this gem is your property?

The gevir replied,

- This stone came into my possession as inheritance from my ancestors.

So the rabbi's daughter asked him,

- And did not your elders find a more worthy place for this stone than the belly of a bird? Our good logic cannot accept such a thing.

Then the daughter added,

- And you, youth, how can you prove that this stone belongs to you. What are the true indications?

The youth replied,

- This stone is mine and I offer proof and signs. It has two exceptional qualities. The first is that one can taste any food

Two Musicians – Mane Katz

he desires if he places it in his mouth. And the second quality is that one can place it on the arm and immediately be lifted into the sky.

The rabbi heard these things but did not believe them. So he called for a man from the shuk to be brought before the bet din. The rabbi asked this man,

- What is the food most beloved to you?

- I love the taste of young fowl cooked in wine. This dish is my favorite of all foods in the world.

Then the rabbi said to him,

- Open your mouth and place this stone under your tongue. Then tell us what you taste.

The man placed the gem under his tongue and behold, he tasted young fowl cooked in wine. He called out,

- I pray you, give me this stone, and I will return it after one week!

Now, the rabbi was afraid to test out the stone regarding the second quality, lest this man might indeed be lifted into the air and carry the stone away with him. And he sent him on his way

After witnessing the wonder of this, the rabbi commanded that the wealthy man return the stone into the possession of the apprentice to whom he was now certain it belonged. And the rabbi said to the youth,

- Here is your stone in your hand. Now half your work day has come and gone, and your employer will surely not pay you salary for today. Therefore, have your afternoon meal with us.

And so he did. He entered the house of the rabbi and sat at the table with the family. At the meal, the youth and the child of the rabbi's daughter gazed one at the other without end. After the thanksgiving grace blessing, the rabbi asked the youth about the stone,

- How did it come into your hands, from what city are you and who are you?

298

Then the youth related all that he had experienced. That he had been seized by an eagle who cast him on the roof of a certain house. And he told all that had taken place from beginning to end. When the daughter of the rabbi heard these things, she fainted and fell to the ground. Immediately her mother and the servants brought spices and fragrance to waken her. Then the rabbi asked the youth,

- My son, do you know how to write your name?

- How could I not know? My father is a great rabbi and I well know how to read and to write. And I am versed in Torah and Gemarra.

The rabbi instructed,

- Write your name on this paper and let us see.

The youth wrote his name and the name of his father. Immediately, the rabbi turned to his daughter,

- Bring your ketuba scroll and let us see.

The scroll was brought and all could see that the youth's handwriting was the very same as the groom's signature on the ketuba. And that his name and the name of his father were also the same as written there. The rabbi became greatly excited.

Then the word went out in the city that the owner of the precious gem, the baker's apprentice, was the son-in-law of the rabbi. They took away his torn clothing and dressed him in fine embroidered linen, and all were joyous. A great feast was prepared on that night and on the next day, as was the custom in that place. All the notables and the sages and the Israelites of the city joined in the celebration to honor the rabbi and his son-in-law; and to honor our well-loved Elijah the Prophet, of excellent merit and fine memory.

After several days, the groom traveled with his wife and her parents to the city of Fez to visit his father. There all rested contentedly in pure harmony and were very happy. All gave praise and thanksgiving to the Creator of the Universe for His abundant blessings and for the miraculous works and wonders which the Blessed Lord had granted them.

This tale was told by the eminent Hahkam Reb' Yosef Morian, of the city of Davduk in the year 1891. It is found in the book by Haim HaLevi Avtar, a resident of Damascus and of Jerusalem, who was a direct descendant of the Jews expelled from Spain in 1492.

The Rebbe's Nigun

This is a tale that Rabbi Naphtali Zevi Ropshitser liked to tell. Once, Rabbi Moshe Leib of Sasov performed the mitzvah of arranging a marriage between two poor orphans, a young man and a young woman. In the instant that the canopy was raised above the heads of the bride and groom, an exquisite luminescence was seen to shine forth from the rebbe's countenance. For as he stood alongside the both bride and groom to make them joyous on the day of their union, he felt himself parent of each.

After the kedushin, Rabbi Moshe Leib danced with exultant energy to the klezmer music. Suddenly, the sweetness of one particular nigun so astounded him that he halted and spoke aloud from the murmurings of his heart,

- Would that this very nigun accompany me on the day I am taken to the place that men all arrive to. The day I am sought after and called up to the celestial dwelling.

Many years passed, and the matter was forgotten.

On the fourth day of the Hebrew month of Shevat in the year of the Creation 5567, it happened that a wedding party was traveling together with a klezmer band to the town of

Brodie. Along their way a terrible snowstorm fell upon them and the horses began to go mad. The wagon descended from the king's road, and the wedding party and musicians began a wild race up slopes and down valleys. The wagon-master was helpless; he was not able to rein in his horses and return them to the straight road.

Wondering what madness had suddenly taken hold to his team which was always obedient, he asked himself the source of this evil inclination. He appeased his horses with kind and soothing talk, then blasphemed and threatened with the whip. He made them feel the force of his anger and then tried good sense – all to no avail.

Whether by reason of the kind words or the scoldings, after a hectic ride the horses calmed and returned at a slow trot to the king's road; but they seemed to take their own direction. Finally the party approached a cemetary where a great funeral was taking place.

The passengers asked,

- What place is this and who is the deceased?

The many people gathered there called out,

- The Zaddik Rabbi Moshe Leib of Sasov has abandoned us and gone from this world!

Then an elderly musician in the wedding party thought of what Rabbi Moshe Leib had requested many years ago. For it was these very klezmers who had played at the wedding of those two poor orphans, and brought joy to the groom and bride on the day of their hupa. And he recalled to all the musicians the nigun which had cast such a sweet awe upon the Zaddik Rebbe that he had risen up and called out,

- Would that this very nigun accompany me on the day of my departure from this life!

So the elder klezmer said to his fellows,

- Come friends, let us play our fiddles and stroke our drums. Pipe your flutes and play the nigun which the rebbe loved so well!

GLOSSARY

A

Ad'mor Title of respect, literally, "Our master and teacher"

Aggadah Homiletic passages in Rabbinic literature

Aleph-bet First two letters and title of Hebrew alphabet

Av bet-din Presiding judge of Rabbinic court of law

Avrech Yeshiva student, usually married

B

Ba'al Shem Tov Rabbi Israel ben Eliezer of Medzibezh. Founder of Hasidic Movement; literally "holder of sacred names of the Almighty"

Ba'al din Litigent

Bachur Bachelor

Bet din Rabbinic court of law

Bet knesset/batei knesset Synagogue/in plural

Bet midrash House of Torah study, also used as place of prayer

Bereshit "In the beginning." Hebrew title of first book of the Bible

Besh't Initials of Rabbi Israel Ba'al Shem Tov

Birkhat hamazon Grace after meals eaten with bread

Brit Mila Circumcision - covenant between Father Abraham and the Almighty. Performed on eight day old male infants

D

Da'at Wisdom, knowledge

Darshan One who exposits holy texts and teaches morals

Dayyan 1) Judgeship in Torah court of law; 2) refers also to the Almighty

Derekh eretz Good manners and respect

Din Torah Judgement by Rabbinic Dayyan

Drasha Homiletic sermon

E

Etrog Citron. One of the four species central to the Feast of the Tabernacles

Erev Eve. A day is considered to begin on the prior evening, upon the sighting of three stars

G

Ga'on Title of respect, literally, "meritorious Torah scholar"

Gan Eden Garden of Eden

Gemarra The second and

supplementary part of the Talmud, providing commentary on the first part - the Mishnah

Gemiluth hesed Benevolence, loving-kindness

Get Divorce according to Jewish Law

Gevir / Gevirim A rich lord, here among the Jews / the plural

H

Hakham A sage-rabbi

Ha-Hozeh The Seer of Lublin, Rabbi Jacob Isaac, a renowned zaddik and miracle worker

Halakhah Legal part of Jewish tradition literature

Hametz Leavened foods, especially breads. Forbidden to Jews during the eight days of Passover

Hasid/hasidim Member of popular religious movement founded by Rabbi Israel Ba'al Shem Tov, which emerged in the 18th century. Distinguished by ecstasy and mass enthusiasm, under the charismatic religious leadership of a "rebbe"

Havdala Benediction over wine, spices and braided candle at the conclusion of the Sabbath, which comforts the soul pained by its parting from the Divine Presence of the Sabbath. [Following festivals, candle and spices are eliminated]

HaMakom "He who is present Everywhere." One of the names of the Almighty

Heder Infant and lower Torah school for boys

"Hoshen Mishpat" Fourth volume of the 'Shulhan Arukh' code of law

Hupa Bridal canopy

K

Kaballah The discipline of Torah-based mysticism

Kadosh Holy; a holy man

Kamea Amulet instilled with mystical properties

Kedosho "Sainted One," manner of addressing venerated rabbi, etc.

Kedushin Marriage; literally the sanctification

Ketuba Marriage contract

Kiddush Benediction over wine on Sabbath eve

Klezmer Jewish folk band, generally with violin

Kolel Yeshiva, usually for married men

Kol nidre Opening liturgical prayer of Yom Kippur Eve

M

Maggid/Maggidim Title of respect, literally "morals preacher". Here, referring especially to several early Hasidic leaders

Ma'ot Talmudic term for money.

"Mapa" "Tablecloth". A scholarly work containing explanations, including customs of Ashkenazi scholars, and added to the "Prepared Table" codification of Jewish law by Joseph Caro

Maran Aramaic, initials for title, "Our teacher, master and rabbi"

Mechubadi Honorable sir

Melave Malka "Accompanying the Sabbath Queen." A fourth festive meal held after the havdala benediction and added to the three Sabbath meals

Minchah Afternoon prayer service

Minyan Required quorum of men for community prayers

Mitzvah/mitzvot Torah precept, good deed/in the plural

Mishnah Collection of Oral Law, compiled by Rabbi Judah Ha-Nasi which forms the basis of the Talmud

Mohel Man performing circumcision

N

A Nigun Specifically, a hasidic melody sung with intense fervor and feeling, especially at the Sabbath or festival table

"No'am Elimelech" Rabbi Elimelech of Lyzhansk, named for his comprehensive work on Zaddikism of that name.

P

Parasang A land measure of between 2.8 to 4.2 miles

Parnass/parnassim Lay leader/in the plural

Pesach Passover

Piyut Liturgical hymn

Posek Rabbinical scholar who pronounces in halahkic disputes

R

Reb' Mister, salutation of respect, usually used with first name

Rebbe Spiritual leader of a group of Hasidim

Rabbenu Our Rabbi. One of several titles expressing both respect and affection

Rebbetzin Wife of a rabbi

Rosh Hodesh The first day of each Hebrew calendar month. Considered a festive day

Rosh Yeshiva Rabbinical head of yeshiva

S

Sabbath/Shabbos Jews are instructed to cease all labor and be joyous on the Seventh day of the week; as the Lord ceased His labors on the seventh day of Creation/ The Ashkenazi pronunciation Hebrew, common among East European

Jews

Sandak Godfather serving infant at circumcision

Seder - The "order" of the Passover table on the first night of the festival when the "Exodus" from Egypt is recalled and celebrated

Seuda Shlishit Third of proscribed Sabbath festive meals

Shadkhan Matchmaker

Shammash Beadle

Shatnez A forbidden mixture of cloth woven from combined wool and linen

Shekhinah The Divine Presence

Shmonah Esre A central prayer recited in the morning, afternoon and evening services

"Shulchan Aruch" "Prepared Table". The authoritative code of Jewish law by Joseph Caro which concentrates on the Sephardi school of halahkic practice

Sitra achra Aramaic term in Kaballah for the "other side," the power of Satan

Sukkoth - Feast of the Tabernacles

T

Tallit Prayer shawl

Talmid hahkam Torah scholar

Talmud Mishnah and Gemarra

Tefillin Phylacteries

Tikkun 1) Purification and correction of a person's soul; 2) Repairing the original downfall of man, which brought about evil and suffering in the world

Tikkun Shabbos Specially composed Sabbath songs and readings

Tikkun hazot A mid-night prayer service

Torah Not only the Five Books of Moses, and by extension the entire Bible, but the whole complex of Jewish learning, comprised of the Talmud, the Commentaries, Rabbinic writing, etc.

Treif Not kosher

V

Vatikin Prayer service conducted at dawn

Y

Yasher ko'ach "All power to you." Usually said in compliment for a well-spoken Torah portion or sermon

Yeshiva Talmudic lower school or college

Yom Kippur The Day of Atonement, the holiest day in the Jewish year

Z

Zaddik The holy man, his thoughts constantly on G-d, who helps to elevate the prayers of his followers, their thoughts and actions. As a channel through which Divine grace flows, he has the power to work miracles

Zeddaka Charity. A central precept in Judaism

Zohar "The book of Splendor", the central work in the literature of the Kaballah. Written in the 13th century